The Head Coach's Playbook

Chris Sherman

ISBN: 0615851096
ISBN-13: 9780615851099

WARNING

This book contains material that may be offensive to some: graphic language, homosexual relations, adult situations, and explicit sexual descriptions.

CONTENTS

ACKNOWLEDGMENTS

Cover photo by Les Byerley

http://www.les3photo8.com

Royalty-free rights obtained through Dreamstime.com.

CHAPTER ONE

Having spent most of a beautiful September Sunday trapped in my home office grading student papers, I decided to take a break and head out for some fun. Fun, however, in this small town is difficult to find, so I headed over to the adult book store in a nearby city to play some video games in the adult arcade and see if anything interesting wandered in off the street.

Arriving at the store, I found the usual assortment of middle-aged trolls milling around the arcade area hoping to pick up some action in the private viewing booths. Some of the booths had glory holes, and it was not uncommon for one or two of the most desperate—and ugly—men to cash in a twenty dollar bill for tokens and take up residence in one of the booths that shared a glory hole. No one in the joint caught my eye, so I dropped a token in one of the video game machines and began what I figured would be a marathon night of Word Dojo.

A few games later, I heard the buzzer out front announce the arrival of a new customer, so I glanced up in the direction of the door to the outer store area. Standing directly across from me was a man I knew all too well. Every morning I stood at my outpost in the school cafeteria and devoured his body with my eyes. Over six feet tall with brown hair, dark skin, and very hairy legs, Carl Harden was the school's head football coach. I had lusted after his well toned body for years without any real hope that I would ever be able to do more than fantasize about touching him. He was, after all, married with two children. His wife worked in our building, and from what I had observed, they were quite happily married. Now here he was standing in the back room of an adult bookstore with a handful of tokens and his trademark khaki cargo shorts revealing those muscular legs. He seemed to be intently studying the signs on the doors to two adjacent booths, trying to decide which trio of porn flicks he wanted to try first. He glanced my way but did not make direct eye contact, then he pulled open the door to one of the glory hole booths and walked inside.

I could not believe this was happening. I had fantasized about having this man's cock in my mouth for at least four years now, and now here he was standing in a booth not ten feet from me, probably with his zipper down and his cock in his hand in full view of the glory hole that opened into the adjacent booth. One part of me wanted to bolt to the booth next door to him and offer to take his cock down my willing throat. But another part of me warned such an act could be a huge mistake. What if I entered the booth only to discover he was not interested. I had never seen him in here before, so maybe he was not even aware of the glory hole when he selected that booth. He had seen me; if I seemed eager to service him and he was repulsed by the act, he could go back and spread word through the entire male faculty about my approaching him. Damn, what to do, what to do.

An older man left the video game behind me and started for the booth adjoining Carl's. No time left for hesitation. If anyone was going to down Carl's load tonight, it was going to be me. I abandoned the video game mid-session and slid into the booth next to Carl just ahead of the troll. I dropped a token in the slot, punched the button until a gay video came onto the screen and then sat down to enjoy my one minute of film. Nonchalantly, I glanced at the glory hole. Through the opening I could see the fabric of Carl's cargo shorts. He was standing right in front of the glory hole, his hand inside the open fly of his shorts, slowly massaging his cock. I bent just enough to be able to see past his leg to the screen in his booth. Straight porn. Shit. He was watching some bimbo with inflated boobs get fucked hard and fast by a young Adonis. Then my view of the screen was obliterated as Carl turned and faced the glory hole. He pulled his cock from the opening in his shorts and began to stroke it with long slow strokes. He was already semi-hard. His hand was wrapped around the shaft and he stroked slowly up and down the length of his cock. It was thick with a large mushroom shaped head and appeared about eight inches in length. I reached out and ran my finger around the inside of the glory hole and then withdrew it and waited. I did not have to wait long. Carl edged forward, guiding his cock through the opening. I fell to my knees and flicked my tongue across the tip a few times before taking his cock in my hand and tilting it upward so I could run my tongue along the underside where the vein swelled noticeably with the lapping of my tongue. I tongued the head of his cock and it jerked upwards in response. Sliding the thick mushroom head into my mouth, I slowly worked my way down his cock until my nose touched the wall and every available inch of his meat was buried in my throat. I began sliding up and down his meat, swirling my tongue along the underside of his cock as I went, varying the strokes to keep him guessing when I would next plunge down on his cock to the base. I could feel him pressing against the flimsy wall that separated us, trying to force more of his rigid cock deeper into my throat. His cock pulsed with each stroke of my tongue and the vein along the underside filled noticeably. I pulled back and tongued the tender flesh around the head of his cock then plunged his dick down my throat until his pubes tickled my face. An audible gasp from the other side of the partition signaled his surprise and approval. I began sucking hard and fast sliding the full length of his shaft, milking that gorgeous thick cock for all it was worth. Then, on a deep plunging down stroke, his hot cum flooded the back of my mouth. I swallowed hard and continued my assault on his cock as another smaller load burst forth, filling my mouth with his salty seed and eliciting a moan from his side of the partition. I continued to work his cock with my mouth until it began to soften and Carl slowly eased it back through the glory hole.

I fumbled in my pocket for a token and dropped it into the slot bringing the screen back to life. I could hear Carl zipping his pants and then the sound of the booth's door opening. His footsteps were rapid as he moved past the door to my booth and headed for the exit. I waited until the screen went black before opening the door to my booth and heading back to the video game I had abandoned. Four games later, I left the arcade area, crossed through the assortment of dildos and porn magazines in the bookstore's front room and headed to my car.

Back at my apartment, I stripped off my clothes and headed to the shower. Carl may have gotten his cock drained, but the experience had left me rock hard and yearning for release. The taste of Carl's jism lingering in my mouth, I stepped into bathroom and turned on the shower. Waiting for the water to warm, I took appraisal of the image reflected in the full length mirror on the back of the bathroom door. I was thirty eight years old, but hours spent in the gym had kept my body taunt and relatively well defined. I kept my hair cut short and dyed a shade lighter than my natural color, or what I vaguely remembered to be my natural color. I had started turning gray before I exited college and found that the dye was worth the mess and aggravation. Regular visits to the tanning bed at the gym kept a warm, healthy glow on my skin, and since I tanned in a bikini, there was always a sharp tan line that pulled attention to my round bubble ass and trimmed groin. Bucking the trend for smooth bodies, I kept my hairy chest trimmed but not shaved. My chest was well developed with sensitive nipples that rose to the occasion every time a man grazed them with his lips or finger. No six pack of abs, but no love handles nor beer gut either, so I felt no shame listing my physique as "athletic" on social networking sites. Born with naturally large, muscular thighs, I did not neglect them in my workout routine and they were perhaps the most ripped part of my body. If I wrapped my legs around a lover, he was not going anywhere, though I had never really had a man who managed to get between my thighs seem to be in a rush to leave.

I stepped into the tub and pulled the shower curtain. The warm water flowed down over my shoulders and felt very welcome after a long day hunched over paperwork. I lathered my body with soap, stepping forward so I could take my time running my hands over my chest and down my thighs, eyes closed, imagining the sensual stroking was being done by someone else's hands. Lathering my cock and balls well, I began to stroke my hardening cock as I replayed the scene from the video booth in my mind. Carl's hairy muscled legs had often been the object of my fantasies and my biggest regret of the night was that the thin plywood wall had separated us and kept me from running my hands up and down his calves and thighs while I buried his cock in my throat. Feeling his cock in my mouth had been wonderful, a dream come true, but still I yearned to explore the rest of his body, to feel his skin beneath my fingertips, to trace his aureoles with my tongue, to feel his hands touching me in the way I was now touching myself. Reaching up to the ledge at the top of the shower, I retrieved a butt plug and began easing it into my ass. I had lubed my hole before going to the bookstore in hopes of finding a willing top man to fill me with his cock, but that had not happened. The residual lubricant eased the way for the plug to enter my ass. I returned my attention to my cock, which was now raging hard and dripping pre-cum. I grasped my shaft and began to milk it slowly, bringing myself to the edge of orgasm, then backing off before resuming my rhythmical stokes. In my mind, Carl's cock was buried deep inside me and his hand was now massaging my shaft as his cock massaged my prostrate. I felt myself getting closer and closer to shooting. The hot water pounded on my back as my ass tightened around the butt plug and my large balls pulled up tight to my groin. I began beating my cock rapidly until at last a hot load shot onto the tub floor. A few strokes later, a second wad oozed from my piss slit and landed on my leg. I leaned against the shower wall for support as my legs felt weak and unstable. Slowly I re-lathered my body, this time to remove the cum that had landed on my legs and feet. I turned to face the pulsating stream of water from the shower head and luxuriated in the last warmth of its caress before shutting off the water and stepping from the tub.

I toweled dry and walked into my bedroom. I double checked the alarm, killed the lights, and slid beneath the clean sheets I had put on the bed earlier in the day. Tomorrow was a work day. I wondered how Carl would react when we met in the hallways at school. Would he avoid me entirely now that we had shared this intimacy? Most married men were hit-and-run artists. Their desire drove them to initiate man-to-man contact, but as soon as their load exited their body guilt usually flooded into its place and they fled the scene of their perceived crime. Carl had made a similar hasty exit from the video booth next to mine once his cock had been drained, and I was unsure how he would handle it the next day. We both had morning cafeteria duty, which meant standing in our appointed stations in the school's cafeteria for twenty minutes before the bell rang for first period and making sure no one started a fight or trashed the place. Our stations were directly across the room from each other, so eye contact was inevitable. Of course, Carl was usually surrounded by two or three of his coaching buddies, so it would be easy for him to avoid looking at me without being blatantly self-conscious about it. How would he handle this new connection we shared? I glanced at the clock: 11:45. In only seven hours, I would find out.

CHAPTER TWO

Monday morning was filled with mixed emotions as I prepared for work. On one hand, I was excited at the prospect of seeing Carl again and ogling his fine physique. On the other hand, if he went out of his way to avoid me or acted like nothing had happened, well, I was not sure I was ready for that kind of rejection.

I arrived at school about ten minutes earlier than usual, slid my name from "out" to "in" on the sign-in board in the main office, collected my mail and headed to my room. I unlocked my door and dropped my stack of papers on my desk next to the laptop, turned on the computer and logged into the attendance program, then locked the keyboard and headed for the cafeteria. Carl was already there and engaged in conversation with Brad, one of his assistant football coaches and a fellow physical education teacher. Brad was about ten years younger than Carl and often acted more like his lackey than his equal. Where Carl was tall, hitting around six feet, four inches, with a lean muscular body, Brad was barely five foot ten and built like a wrestler, which he had been in high school. Brad had brown, curly hair that he wore just below his collar—it was the kind of hair women envy and gay men envision grasping during rough sex. Both wore the PE department's trademark khaki cargo shorts—replete with pockets to house whistles, pass pads, and stopwatches. Brad's hairy legs were much thicker than Carl's but just as firm and inviting to a man like me who loves to caress some hairy legs while draining a hard cock.

I walked past them on my way to my assigned location, intentionally not looking in their direction. From what I could gather, the subject was football. Go figure. Students milled around the tables, some having gotten their breakfast and looking for a place to eat it in relative peace, others looking for friends with whom to congregate and catch up on everything that had happened since they last text messaged each other in the parking lot. I tried not to stare in Carl's direction, instead focusing on the door leading from the serving line which allowed me to watch him out of my peripheral vision. He stood with his back and one leg against the wall, balancing on his left leg with his hands behind his back. Brad stood at an angle in front of him and seemed to be dominating the conversation. Finally the bell for first period rang and students began moving from the tables toward the exit leading to the academic wing. Brad continued to chatter, but Carl had changed his stance and his sightline. I could feel his eyes on me, so I glanced in his direction. He raised his eyebrows and smiled, then his right hand slid to his crotch and adjusted his junk. Less than a second later, he was moving across the cafeteria toward the gym doors, Brad at his heels. Message received.

I don't remember much about the rest of that day or the day that followed it, but on Wednesday of that week I arrived to school to find a message from Carl waiting in my email inbox: "Can we meet in my office today during your planning period to discuss Jason Durham's grades? Colleges are scouting him this season, but he will not get a scholarship if he continues to make poor grades in his core subjects. I would like to devise an after-school study plan for him."

My planning period did not happen until third period, right before lunch. I could barely concentrate on teaching the history of Greek theatre without my mind wondering to other activities the Greek men were reputed to enjoy. Three long, tedious hours later the bell rang ending second period. I printed out a copy of Jason Durham's grades and a list of his missing assignments. All the way down the corridor I kept telling myself that Carl was only interested in making sure his star player remained eligible to play and did not end up flunking my class before the season ended. But those raised eyebrows and that Michael Jackson crotch grab gave me hope that there was more than grades on the coach's mind.

All of the male PE teachers shared one large office right off of the gym, so that was where I went. When I opened the door, however, Carl was not there. Jamie Myers, the baseball coach, sat at his cubicle entering grades into his school-issued laptop. He did not bother to look up when I entered, probably assuming it was another PE teacher. "Do you know where I could find Coach Harden?"

"Yeah. He's probably in the football office."

"Where is that?"

"Down the side hall, on the left just past the entrance to the team room."

"Thanks." I started to turn to the door, but at that moment he finally looked up from his screen and made eye contact. Beautiful blue eyes in a face that probably wouldn't stop a clock, but it would definitely slow it down. His eyes, though a beautiful shade of blue, were close set beneath a brow that could have been used as a bookshelf. His nose was wide and had been broken so many times in college that it looked like a roadside sign warning of dangerous curves ahead.

"If you don't find him there, check out on the field. He sometimes goes down there to make sure the turf has been repaired when we have a home game coming up."

"Will do. Thanks again."

"Anytime," he said as he turned back to the screen and began punching keys with one finger. I took a last look and then turned to the door. Apparently aware that his face would not be his selling point, Jamie Meyers had invested heavily in developing a trim body that would pull both men and women's eyes away from his gap-toothed smile. He was tall, thin with a washboard stomach that probably could have been called a twelve pack. He wore his clothes skin tight to make sure everyone knew every muscle group in his body was sharply defined. Seated, he had deprived me of a good view of his bubble butt, but I knew from following him down the hall on numerous occasions that his ass was probably his best feature.

I left the gym and turned down a side hallway that led to the health classroom on one side and the team room on the other. Just beyond the team room door I found what I supposed was the football office though there was no placket outside the door to verify that fact. I knocked on the door and heard Carl's muffled voice tell me to come on in. The room was larger than I had expected. Carl sat at a large desk that had been pushed up against the wall in one corner. A single chair bridged the space between the side of the desk and the door through which I had just entered. The opposing wall played host to a large overstuffed cream colored loveseat, obviously a cast-off from someone's apartment. Carl followed my eyes to the love seat and offered, "I brought that in here when we got a new living room set. On game days I try to catch a nap in the afternoon. Otherwise Friday becomes one hell of a long day. "

"Makes sense." I was surprised how easily we were conversing. There was none of that awkwardness I had feared might dominate the meeting.

"Have a seat."

I dropped onto the lone chair beside his desk and nervously crossed my legs so I could balance the papers I had brought with me on my lap. Carl sat facing me with his right leg crossed over his left knee. Damn, I wanted to play with those hairy legs! Carl did not say anything, so I motioned to the papers on my lap. "Jason is extremely lazy. The work is not that difficult and he has ample time in class to complete his assignments, but he wastes the bulk of his time covertly trying to look up his statistics on his smart phone."

He leaned back in his chair and clasped his hands behind his head. "That's not a big surprise. He always wants to goof off during practice too. He is one of those kids for whom the skills of the game come naturally and he doesn't see a need to work at it. I've spoken to him numerous times, but he just doesn't seem to understand that he has to practice like it is game day if he wants his teammates to play well in the game. He's damned good on the field, but he is no leader for the team. That's why I want to put the screws to him."

Did he really just say that?

He continued, "The only thing that matters to him is the social aspect of practice sessions, so that is what I plan to take away. I am going to make him sit in one of the health rooms and complete all of his assignments each day before he can join the team on the practice field. One of the assistant coaches will be there to monitor him and make sure he is actually doing his own work."

"Sounds like a plan," I said, handing him the printout of Jason's current grades. "I also brought copies of the assignments he is missing." I slid those onto the desk in front of him.

"Good."

He dropped his hands into his lap and hiked his shorts up a few inches. The effect was obvious. The outline of his cock was clear as it lay against his left leg. His eyes never broke contact with mine, but his hand started caressing his thickening member through his shorts. "I also wanted to thank you," he said.

"No problem. We all have to work together to get Jason through this year."

"That's not why I want to thank you." His gaze dropped meaningfully to his lap and then returned to lock eyes with mine. "You're very good at what you do." He grinned, then added, "And I was hoping you might want to practice that skill more often."

"You know what they say—practice makes perfect."

"Indeed," he quipped as he rose from his chair and reached across me to lock the door. Standing directly in front of me now, he slowly unbuckled his belt, and unbuttoned the waistband of his cargo shorts. I reached out to assist him with the zipper, and within seconds his shorts and jock strap were crumpled around his ankles and his semi-erect cock was bobbing in front of my face. I leaned forward and flicked my tongue across the tip of his cock, and it jerked in response. I grabbed his shaft to hold it steady as I guided it between my lips. Carl reached behind me with his right hand and ran his fingers through my hair until he had a firm grasp on the back of my head, then he gently but firmly pulled my face forward until his cock slid down my throat and my nose was buried in his pubes. I began to slurp his meaty cock, sliding up and down the shaft in a slow, steady rhythm. His hand on the back of my head allowed me to withdraw until only the head of his cock remained in my mouth, then he would push against my head to propel me back to the base of his throbbing shaft. I eagerly tongued the engorged vein on the underside of his cock. He was horned, and it was obvious this would not take long. He was almost ready to cum and we had barely gotten started. His grip relaxed on the back of my head, and I began to swirl my tongue around his cock. His cock had gotten thicker and it was more difficult now for me to do much more than slide up and down on his rigid cock. I reached behind him and grasped his ass cheeks in my hands and gave them a squeeze as I slammed up and down on his big dick, each time my forehead slapping his taunt stomach. I stroked the back of his legs and felt them tense up as he rose onto the balls of his feet and leaned further into me. I could taste his precum in the back of my throat and I wanted to feel that jet of sperm as it filled my mouth the way it had Sunday night in the bookstore. I began sucking harder, faster, applying more pressure on the vein with my tongue. I could hear his breathing become more rapid and feel the muscles in his body tense. He was close to shooting, and I knew it.

"Unbutton your shirt," he gasped. It seemed a strange request, but when the man about whom you have been fantasizing for over two years says to unbutton your shirt, you do it. It was difficult to accomplish with his cock slamming in and out of my mouth and his body pressed tightly against mine, but I managed to get all of the buttons free and pulled my shirt open from neck to waist. The precum was becoming more abundant and I was sure he was going to explode any moment when he suddenly grasped his cock with his left hand and pulled it out of my mouth. He pushed down on his shaft and a hot bolt of jism flew from his cock and landed on my breastbone. He leaned forward and pushed his cock through my waiting lips just in time for the second blast to fill my mouth with his thick saltiness.

"Don't swallow," he directed in a whisper as his body relaxed. He held his cock in my mouth while I slowly, gently sucked the last drops of semen from his softening member. He pulled his cock free and bent down and planted his lips on mine. I was shocked by the suddenness of this move, and he slipped his tongue inside my mouth. His lips pressed hard against mine as he explored my mouth with his tongue. I could feel his right hand rubbing the hair on my chest from center to the right, then back across to my left nipple which he took between thumb and forefinger and applied slight pressure.

"Nipples sensitive?"

"Very."

"Good. I'll remember that for next time." He bent over and pulled open the bottom desk drawer and extracted a small white hand towel. He used it to clean his cock and then dropped it on top of his desk. "I love to taste my cum inside another man's mouth," he whispered as he pulled his jock strap up and adjusted his cock inside the pouch. "Rarely get to do that at the bookstore."

I reached for the towel on his desk to clean off the cum he had smeared across my chest. His hand shot out to stop me. "Leave it. It will dry in a few minutes and you can button your shirt without worrying about it making wet spots. I want you to go through the rest of this day with the taste of my seed in your mouth and knowing it is matted onto your chest. It'll be our secret that no one else in the building would ever suspect."

A few minutes later I emerged from the football office and headed back to my classroom. In the hallway I was met by Jamie Myers with a stack of papers in his hand. He was heading in the direction of the health rooms. "Did you find Coach Harden?" he asked as he came closer.

"Sure did," I quipped.

"Cool," he replied offhandedly as he turned into one of the classrooms.

No, I thought, hot. Definitely hot.

CHAPTER THREE

I did not hear anything from Carl for nearly a week. Every morning we stood across the cafeteria from each other, and while there was no concerted effort not to make eye contact, neither of us pushed the envelope to make an obvious connection. Carl continued to have Brad or one of the other assistant coaches engaged in a conversation, so the situation never felt awkward—just two men who happened to know a secret and knew better than to give any outward signs of such knowledge. Then, on Tuesday of the week following our meeting in his office I received another email. The message was a bit cryptic: "I need your assistance with a project tomorrow during planning period. Can you meet me in the press box to the gym at 11:15? Come clean."

"Come clean?" What in hell was that supposed to mean? Well, there was only one way to find out—show up the next day at 11:15. The time struck me as odd—not the beginning of the period, but nearly twenty minutes into the period. Perhaps he had something else he had to do first. I was hoping his demand that I "come clean' was an indication he wanted to move beyond the oral gratification I had now given him on two occasions. Nothing would make me happier than for him to force that hefty cock of his into my tight ass and ride it until his seed exploded inside of me. I imagined what it would feel like to have his bare chest pressed against my back and his hands grasping my waist as he plunged deeper and deeper inside of me. I imagined his strong thighs and muscular ass tensing as he rode harder and harder. And I longed to feel the weight of his body collapse on top of me once he finished and his body went slightly numb from the sudden relaxation of his muscles which had been tensing up throughout the act.

That night I ate practically nothing and spent nearly a half hour in the shower with an enema bottle flushing myself in preparation for what I was hoping might happen the next day. The following morning I awoke early to go through the entire process again. "Come clean," he had demanded. I planned to make sure I delivered. Standing in the shower forcing warm water up my rectum, I found myself thinking, if straight women had to go through everything gay men put themselves through in order to have sex, there would be a hell of a lot fewer unplanned pregnancies. Finally satisfied that my asshole could pass an OSHA inspection, I toweled off and dressed for work. Pulling open my underwear drawer, I surveyed the options. I wanted something that he would find alluring, but I did not want to come across as too feminine. Carl had a woman at home, so he did not want or need another female. Boxers were out—too conservative. Briefs I did not own. Bikinis and thongs would be too feminine in his eyes. What was left? The man was an athlete—go for the obvious. I pulled a red jockstrap from the drawer and pulled it into place. It would provide the control I would need during cafeteria duty that morning when I had to stand there and watch his beautifully toned body and anticipate what might happen later. The last thing I needed was to throw a boner in the cafeteria, so the jockstrap would be a good choice and help hold my errant dick hostage should the situation try to arise. I turned to catch a profile image in the mirror, and I liked what I saw. The red contrasted nicely with the deep tan on my legs and torso and highlighted the creamy whiteness of my un-tanned ass cheeks. The look was masculine, but inviting. I grinned. I would definitely do me. Hopefully Carl would too.

Carl and Brad were already in place at his post in the cafeteria when I arrived that morning. Carl normally had a mug of coffee in one hand, but this morning he was holding a large paper cup from a local fast food chain renowned for their fruit smoothies. Avoiding direct eye contact, I found myself staring at his legs, admiring the thick fur that covered them, the curve of tight muscle that defined his calf. My eyes traveled slowly up his body. H e was wearing basketball shorts and a t-shirt that clung to his torso and left no doubt to the rippling muscle definition beneath the flimsy cloth. His arms were deeply bronzed from hours in the sun and covered in a less dense version of the fur on his legs. He slowly raised his smoothie to his lips and sipped from the straw.

His eyes made direct contact with mine and locked. His lips slid from the straw, and he licked his upper lip with a slow arc of his tongue, raised his right eyebrow and then winked. He folded his arms across his chest, his right hand still holding the smoothie, his left hand subtly fingering his right nipple. Brad continued talking to him without seeming to notice that Carl's attention was elsewhere. Feeling more than just emotion stir in my pants, I broke the gaze and studied the lush green grass of the practice fields beyond the huge windows. Two students were passing a soccer ball to kill the time before the bell rang. They were slender and agile, and for a moment I envied their youth, all the time and possibilities that lie before them. Then I remembered myself at their age—the uncertainty, insecurity, and self-doubt—and I knew I would never trade my knowledge gained from experience for their potential. The stirring in my groin had calmed and I figured it was safe to look back in Carl's direction. He tapped Brad on the shoulder and nodded in my direction. Brad turned and looked unabashedly, smiled, then turned back to Carl. What the fuck was that about, I wondered. The bell rang and students began to scatter. Carl and Brad walked leisurely toward the gym doors, and I passed them on my way to the academic wing of the building. Just as we passed, Carl raised his glass and slurped noisily from the straw. Behind me, I heard him say, "mighty tasty. Thick and creamy, just the way I like it," and I was pretty sure he wasn't talking about the smoothie.

Nothing makes time pass more slowly than anticipation, and I thought the first two block periods of that day would never end. When the bell rang at the end of second period, I still had nearly twenty minutes to kill before our appointed time for meeting, so I pulled up the school website on the computer and did some snooping. Brad had graduated from a local high school before going to an in-state university on a wrestling scholarship. His profile page indicated he had been teaching in the system for only five years, so that would make him about twenty-seven. Carl had graduated from the same local high school, but much earlier than Brad and had attended an out-of-state university on a football scholarship. He had taught for a few years in another state before returning to his hometown. I wondered if Brad's obvious idol worship of Carl had started when the two ended up teaching in the same department at this school or if it had begun much earlier as a younger athlete's envy of the high school's most celebrated graduate. Whatever the connection, one thing was clear: Brad would do anything Carl asked of him.

Locking my keyboard, I headed for the press box. The athletic hall opened off of the cafeteria and ran along one side of the gymnasium. The door to the press box was located about halfway down the hall on the right, only about twenty feet from the door to the football office. I tried the door and found it was unlocked. The door opened onto a narrow space filled by a steep stairway that went straight up in front of the door. At the top of the stairs, I found myself alone in the empty press box. A long counter occupied the wall next to the gym. Above the counter plywood attached to a series of pulleys covered the opening to the gym. Originally the area had been filled by sliding glass windows, but an overzealous sophomore had slammed a basketball up against the glass and broken it, causing the principal to demand the glass be removed and replaced with something more substantial. The building trades teacher had been called to the scene and tasked with rigging a replacement system. When the plywood was hoisted into a raised position, the countertop ledge of the press box opened about three feet above the heads of spectators sitting in the top row of the bleachers. Other than sound equipment at one end of the counter and a half dozen folding chairs, the space was empty. The sound of students engaged in multiple volleyball games sent a cacophony of sound throughout the gym. Soon I heard footsteps on the stairs and turned to see Carl emerge from below. To my surprise, Brad followed him. Carl had a sly grin on his face as he approached me.

“I brought company. I hope you won’t mind.”

Brad hung back and seemed less than comfortable with the situation. A slight blush was on his tanned face and he avoided making direct eye contact with me or Carl. Both hands were rammed into his cargo shorts and the tension was palpable. Carl, however, gave no sign of being tense or concerned about Brad’s unease. Instead, he positioned himself directly in front of me and slid his thumbs under the elastic waistband of his shorts. “Shall we?” he asked with a grin as he slid his shorts down over his thighs and let them drop to the floor. I had not been expecting an audience and was not real comfortable with the situation, but I went down on my knees anyway and reached out to pull Carl’s jockstrap down. His cock sprang free; it was already semi-hard, so I leaned forward and licked the tip of it with my tongue. Carl moaned slightly and his cock twitched, jerking slightly upward at my touch. I parted my lips and encircled his bulbous cock head with my mouth, swirling my tongue around the underside as I slowly slid down his shaft, taking all of his cock down my throat. Carl placed his hands lightly on the top of my head as I began to work his cock.

"When I was in college, there was this guy on my hallway in the dorm who had the hots for me," Carl said. I was unsure if he was talking to me or to Brad, or both. "He was gay and made no secret of the fact that he was willing to service me. I turned him down several times when he would offer to suck me off in the showers, but then one night I came back from a date that had not gone well. She had gotten me really horned up and then wouldn't put out, so when I came in that night I was drunk off my ass and hornier than hell. So I stripped off my clothes and was going to just jerk off in my room, but when I went to get into my bed, I realized my roommate had his girlfriend in the top bunk with him, and I did not want them to think I was lying there jerking off beneath them. So I grabbed my towel and headed to the showers. It was an old dorm, so no one had private bathrooms. It was just one big communal room, so anyone taking a shower was on display. It was nearly two in the morning by then, so I figured no one else would be coming into the bathroom. But as I stood there with the water running over me beating the hell out of my soaped-up cock, this guy walks in the room. He didn't say a word to me. He just walked over into the spray of the shower and dropped to his knees and started to tug on my cock with me. Then he removed my hand from my cock and pushed me backward so the water would spray down and rinse the soap from my cock. Then he took my cock in his mouth and he started to suck it, and I swear to God I thought I had died and gone to heaven. No female had ever sucked my cock like that man did, and when I blew my load down his throat, it was so intense I thought my legs were going to buckle and send me to the floor. We never said a word to each other that night, but from then on if I needed release, I would just go knock on his door and then head to the shower."

His cock was throbbing hard and I was working it for all it was worth. I pulled back and flicked my tongue across the tip of his cock, then slid my tongue down the underside of the shaft and nuzzled my face against his balls. I pulled one of his large balls into my mouth and tongued it, then released it and turned my attention to the other nut.

"I told Brad here that he did not know what he was missing if he had never gotten his cock sucked by a man. No woman can suck a cock like a man can. They are always too hesitant, too gentle, too repulsed. But a man knows what makes himself feel good, so he knows how to make another man feel the same."

I took Carl's cock back into my mouth. The salty taste of his precum oozed into my mouth and I knew it would not be long until he would be ready to give me a load.

"Pull it out," Carl directed, and out of the corner of my eye I saw Brad unbutton his pants and obey. "Come on over here. He doesn't bite, just suck." Brad, pants around his ankles, managed the few awkward steps to bring him side by side with Carl. Carl lifted his hands from my head and backed away enough to release his cock from my mouth. "You don't mind helping my buddy out, do you?" he queried with that tone that said this was not a question but a demand. Obligingly, I slid sideways so that Brad's cock was in front of me. Brad was already rock hard. His cock was not as long as Carl's nor as thick in girth, but it was still a nice cock, about seven inches long. I leaned toward him and wrapped my right hand around the shaft. Lowering my mouth onto the head of his cock, I heard him audibly gasp at the sensation of a warm, wet tongue caressing his cock head. I flicked the tip of my tongue against the underside of his cock at that tender spot where the head and the shaft meet. His hands flew to my shoulders and gripped them hard. I was enjoying his virgin reaction, so I slammed my mouth down to the base of his cock and took it down my throat in one fluid motion that caught him by surprise and caused him to cry out. Brad slapped his right hand over his mouth, but continued his death grip on my shoulder with his left hand as I slid rapidly up and down his shaft. The vein on the underside of his cock bloated with cum almost immediately, so I backed off and released his cock for a moment and turned my attention to his hairy balls. When I took the first one into my mouth, he gasped again and I could feel his legs tremble under my touch as I clasped the backs of his hairy thighs and gently pulled the hairs on his legs as I stroked down the back of his thigh to his ankle and then lightly grazed his skin with my fingertips all the way back up his legs. Releasing his balls, I returned my attention to his cock, teasing the piss slit with my tongue and flicking my tongue across the tip and around the rim of his cockhead before deepthroating his cock once more. Carl stood nearby, watching and pumping his cock with his hand. I slurped and sucked Brad's cock with rapid strokes to bring him back to the edge of orgasm. When I thought he was about to explode, I pulled back from his cock to keep him from shooting just yet. When Brad's cock popped from my mouth, Carl intervened.

"Brad, sit up on the counter, so he can get to you easier," Carl directed. "And you are way too overdressed for this party," he said to me, "Strip." I pulled my polo shirt over my head and dropped it on the counter, then slid my dress slacks down and added them to the pile. "Nice," Carl said as he reached out and ran a finger under the elastic strap of my jockstrap. He pulled it out about two inches from my leg and released it. "Spread those legs, Brad. The man needs room to work," Carl directed. Brad complied and I moved between his legs and took his cock into my mouth once more. Behind me I heard Carl open one of the drawers in the small cabinet in the room and then step behind me. He grabbed my exposed ass cheeks with both hands and squeezed, then released them and slapped first one and then the other playfully.

"My one regret from college is that I never did this," he said. If I had any doubt what "this" was, that was soon erased when I felt his hand spread my ass cheeks and smear lubricant on my hole. He inserted a finger slowly and began to finger fuck me while I pumped Brad's cock with my mouth. "You're clean, aren't you?" Carl asked. I was not sure how I was supposed to answer that question with my mouth full of cock. "Neg, right?" he added. I released Brad's cock long enough to affirm that I was clean and had tested negative only last month. "Good," he almost purred, "cause I don't like wearing a condom." I felt his cock head push against the crack of my ass and I spread my legs further apart to accommodate him as he found the spot and began to push. His cock slid into my hole with ease and I rammed back against him to take every inch of it. "Eager little fucker, aren't you?" he laughed softly and began to fuck my tight hole with a steady rhythm. His hands were on my waist and each thrust of his hips buried my face deeper against Brad's pubes. I placed my hands on the counter's edge to brace myself and allowed Carl's thrusts to dictate my movement up and down Brad's cock. "Damn, this is good," Carl whispered hoarsely, "you enjoying it, Brad?" Brad had verbalized nothing above moans and gasps since arriving in the press box, and the most he could muster now was "yes," which escaped his lips combined with a gasp as I drove his cock even further down my throat.

"Oh my God," Brad whispered, sounding scared. "I'm gonna cum. I'm gonna cum!" He began trying to push my head back off of his cock, but I would not budge.

"Hold off as long as you can," Carl instructed, and he began to pound his cock into my ass deep and hard.

"Oh, Oh, OH!" Brad gasped and I could tell by the way his cock suddenly tensed and the vein throbbed that he was about to send his hot seed flooding down my throat. Seconds later, he released his grip on my shoulder and I could tell he was biting the side of his hand to keep from making any noise as his load erupted and filled my mouth with its sweet and salty seed. Carl was pumping my ass rapidly now and the sound of skin slapping skin was loud enough to echo in the empty room. I continued to milk Brad's cock with my mouth as his dick slowly softened.

"Here it comes," Carl announced as he slammed his cock deep into my gut and his legs began to shake as wave after wave of sperm shot from his cock. I began contracting and releasing my ass muscles to milk every last drop from his big dick, and his grip on my waist tightened to the point it was painful. He kept his dick implanted inside me for a full minute after he had finished, and it was still rock hard when he pulled it out and his semen began oozing from my hole and running down the inside of my leg.

"How do you do that?" he asked as he began wiping his cock with the hand towel he had stored in the drawer with the lube.

"Do what? I asked.

"What you just did with your ass muscles. How the fuck do you do that?"

"Practice. Like everything else, practice makes perfect. There are exercises to work that part of the body just like any other part."

Carl tossed Brad the hand towel, and Brad slid off the counter to a standing position and began to clean his groin. When he was done, he handed the towel to me and I swiped it across my ass cheeks. I did not make an attempt to clean the cum from my inner thighs where it had seeped after Carl withdrew his cock. I personally liked the sensation of having my asshole dripping wet as I walked around following such an encounter, and I knew that Carl would want me to have the dried semen on me for the rest of the day. Like a dog marking his territory, Carl enjoyed knowing he had left his mark. He got off on dominating another man—whether on the playing field or during intercourse—and his dried cum on my thighs served as a trophy of his conquest. We dressed in silence. Gathering up the towel and the lubricant and stuffing them into a small pouch he had also concealed in the drawer, Carl turned to Brad and grinned.

"I told you he was good, didn't I? How was your first blowjob from a man, virgin boy?"

Brad blushed deep red, then replied, "It was great." Carl turned and started down the stairs with Brad traipsing along behind him. When he got to the bottom of the steps, Carl threw open the door and headed back in the direction of his office. Brad suddenly turned and for the first time made eye contact with me. "Thanks," he said. "I mean it. It was fantastic. Watching him . . ." his voice faltered, "Wow, that was hot." He stood there for an awkward moment holding the door with one hand and staring into my eyes without saying anything more, then he turned quickly and rushed down the hall and through the door to the gym. It was then I realized why Carl had wanted to meet twenty minutes after the start of classes. Carl and I had the same planning period, but Brad was supposed to be teaching a physical education class during this period. It was common practice for P. E. teachers to combine classes when they were in the gym and only one of them monitor the student activity while the others worked on paperwork or coaching duties. During the week they would rotate so that each teacher pulled a turn as monitor. Today had been Brad's day to leave his class in someone else's hands. He had to be there to take roll and monitor the boys' locker room at the beginning and the end of the period, so that had been the reason for the delayed meeting in the press box. Clearly Carl had planned this encounter well in advance, for he had stashed the lubricant and hand towel in the drawer, made sure the door was unlocked, and timed the event so he could command Brad's presence. I wondered how many days he had spent planting the notion in Brad's head. I suspected Brad and I were both being used as pawns to fulfill Carl's personal fantasies, but as long as it meant I was going to get Carl's hard cock down my throat and up my ass, that was just fine by me.

CHAPTER FOUR

I overslept the following morning, so I was running late to work, and Carl was already at his station in the cafeteria when I arrived. I had full intentions of just walking past him without acknowledging his presence like I normally did, but he reached out and grabbed my arm as I passed by him. "Hold up," he grinned. He was alone for once, and I wondered why Brad was not in his usual place vying for Carl's undivided attention. "What do you have planned for Sunday afternoon?" Carl asked, ramming his hands down in the pockets of his cargo shorts.

"Nothing special. Why?"

"A couple of us are getting together over at Jamie's place to watch the football game. You should join us if you can."

I studied Carl's face for covert messages, but saw none. Was this really just an invitation to join the clique for an afternoon of male bonding over a football game and some beer? Considering each time I had been invited to join Carl for something he had upped the ante, male bondage seemed more likely than male bonding. Still, I was curious. Just what the hell did he have in mind? Since there was only one way to find out, I shrugged my shoulders and said, "Sure. What time and what address?"

"We usually get together around two in the afternoon. I'll have

Jamie email you the address. Bring a bag of chips and some beer with you. It'll be loads of fun."

We stood there for a few minutes in awkward silence watching the parade of students file through the food service line.

"Jason doing any better at getting his work completed in class?" Carl asked at last.

"Yeah, he is putting forth more effort, but he is easily distracted. All I have to do is say the word 'bench' to get him back on track though."

Carl laughed. "He didn't think we would actually bench his ass until it happened last week. When I put a sophomore into the game in his position, I think that got our message across to him. He's been putting a lot more effort into practices this week."

That was when Brad appeared, walking quickly and slightly out of breath. "Hey there!" He greeted me like he was shocked to find me in this location. "How is it going?"

"Not badly."

"I got all of the new equipment moved from the loading dock to the team room."

"Good," Carl responded, "We can have the strength training class help unpack it and put it away this morning during first block. Guess who is joining us on Sunday?" Carl nodded in my direction, and Brad's face lit up in a huge smile.

"That's awesome! Jamie has a great townhouse with really comfy furniture and a huge HD television screen that takes up almost one entire wall in the living room."

"Are you sure you'll be there, Brad? Will the fiancé let you come?" Carl teased.

Brad blushed a deep red. "She does not control me. We don't have that kind of relationship. Besides, she's gonna be out of town this weekend. She's visiting one of her college roommates and they are going shopping in New York."

"Ahh," Carl intoned, "The truth comes out! The cat is away, so the mouse can play!" He laughed and threw a pseudo punch at Brad's bicep.

"I'll be there," Brad replied, staring Carl down. The he shifted his gaze to me and added, "Trust me." For a man who had avoided eye contact with me at all costs the day before, Brad sure was delivering full, unabashed contact that morning. I wondered what had caused the change. The bell cut our conversation off at that point and we parted ways.

Around the middle of my second block class, the door to my classroom opened and Jamie Myers strode across the front of the room to my desk. My students were busy churning out two major essays on a test. The kids looked up to see who had entered and then resumed writing at a feverish pace. A trio of girls near my desk stared a bit longer than the rest as Jamie crossed the room, but once he neared their desks, they dropped their eyes and resumed writing.

"Hey," he whispered as he neared my desk. "I looked through the window in the door and it didn't look like you were lecturing or anything. Hope I'm not interrupting."

"Nah. They're busy failing a test. Whatcha need?"

"Wanted to bring you this." He thrust a slip of paper toward me. I reached out and took it from him and looked down at the handwriting scrawled across the half sheet of spiral notebook paper. It was an address and a phone number. "I'm over in Lakewood. You shouldn't have any trouble finding it, but in case you do, there's my cell number. Just give me a call and I'll talk you through the streets."

He was close enough that our arms were touching, and he was leaning in conspiratorially as if trade secrets were being exchanged. I suddenly became very conscious of his chiseled chest and abs pressing against the thin lycra fabric of his skin-tight shirt. His aftershave was fresh and clean smelling, very mild, yet quite alluring.

"Thanks. I'm looking forward to it. Is there anything in particular that you want me to bring?"

"Not really, Everyone sort of brings what they like, and then we just pig out on whatever is there. Carl usually shows up with a bag of Doritos. Brad stops by the grocery store down the road and grabs some corn chips and salsa. If I have time, I'll make a seven layer dip, but if not, it'll be potato chips and pretzels. I'm afraid it's not a very classy affair." Jamie straightened up , and I realized he was actually quite tall, or he sure as hell looked tall from my vantage point.

"Sounds like my kind of crowd," I said, flashing him a smile that I hoped did not send the wrong impression. I was still unsure just how much Jamie knew about what had been happening with Carl and I. Carl's invitation this morning had seemed innocent enough, but that "loads of fun" comment felt heavy with innuendo. For all I knew these guys might have a standing tradition of getting together on Sundays under the pretext of watching a game when in fact they were having a good old fashioned circle jerk. The fact that Carl nor Brad had made any attempt at reciprocation the day before led me to believe they were not in the habit of sucking cock themselves, but I had been around enough straight jocks during high school to know that mutual masturbation was not uncommon in that set.

"Well, I'll let you get back to work," Jamie said as he turned and headed for the door. The trio of girls raised their heads and watched him until the door closed behind him. One of them realized I was watching them watch him and turned beet red. She shot the other two a look, and all three stifled a giggle and resumed writing.

When all of the class had finished the test and deposited their essays in the wire basket that sat on the corner of my desk, there were fewer than five minutes left in the period, so I told them they could talk quietly and we would begin the new unit next class period. I pulled a test response from the basket and began grading. The trio of girls nearest my desk began whispering amongst themselves about God only knows what. When it became apparent that I was not paying them any attention, their voices crept up and bits and pieces of the conversation floated my way. I had learned a long time ago that if I pretended not to be listening, I could learn a hell of a lot about what was going on in my students' lives.

"That body!" I heard one girl say.

"Yeah, but that face," another responded.

"Still," the first voice responded, "that body."

"I'd do him," the third voice announced, then added, "Just so long as I didn't have to look at his face."

It didn't take a rocket scientist to know who they were discussing. Jamie Myers had the body of an Adonis, and a face that was easily forgettable. He kept his sandy blonde hair trimmed close to his head and rarely smiled. He had been raised as a farm boy in Pennsylvania and worked on road construction crews during his summers off from college in order to pay his own way. He had never said his parents were dirt poor, but the stories he had told in the teacher's lunchroom left little doubt that he was no stranger to hard work, sweat, and dirt. When a local farmer spread manure on a nearby field one spring and the odor wafted through the open lunchroom windows, a fellow teacher had crinkled her nose and complained about the stench of cow shit. At which point, Jamie Myers had raised his head from his sandwich, inhaled deeply, and said, "No, that's pig crap. There's a big difference."

Myers was clearly self-conscious of his appearance. He barely opened his mouth when he spoke. When he laughed, he covered his mouth with his hand. Both his top and bottom teeth set about a quarter inch apart in the front, a space big enough to insert a pencil. I suspected his parents had never invested in braces because there was no money for such an extravagance. Lack of health insurance and ready cash I guessed was also the story behind his crooked nose. Jamie had been teaching about ten years, so I figured he had not made any attempt to fix the nose or the teeth because money was still tight. He was single, and living alone in a townhouse in this area of the state was not cheap. Most single teachers at the school opted for roommates to share the expenses, but Jamie came across as something of a loner most of the time and only seemed to open up when he was around the teachers in his department. Yet here he was giving me his address and phone number so I could join what was clearly a boys club meeting at his townhouse on Sunday afternoon. I still was not sure if Sunday would be spent watching football—which I detest—or balling, but either way, I wanted to see what these guys were like when they were on a different turf.

The rest of the day passed uneventfully, and Friday brought a nervous excitement to the building. That night would be the first district match for the football team, and it was a home game to boot. Classes were cut short and everyone was rounded into the gymnasium for the last half hour of the day for a pep rally. Cheerleaders jumped and flipped. Football players swaggered across the gym floor as their names were announced, and the band played the same damn song over and over just like they did at every game. Carl addressed the crowd and spoke of the hard work and dedication the team had shown in the preseason games. His assistant coaching staff stood in a line against the wall behind him, hands clasped behind them, looking as relaxed as a row of prisoners facing execution before a firing squad. I commented o n their rigid posture to the teacher standing next to me, and she responded sarcastically, "They train them to do that. It's the only way they can keep them from scratching their balls in public." Finally, the misery came to an end and students rushed from the gym to their cars and the long row of yellow cheese wagons that lined the bus loop. I went home and stripped off my dress clothes and pulled on a square cut bathing suit. I spent the rest of the evening submerged in the hot tub that dominated my postage stamp back yard, a glass of wine in one hand and a novel in the other.

Saturday was dedicated to cleaning the house, doing laundry, hitting the gym, and then curling up on the sofa with my beagle. The movie was a sleeper and soon so was I. I awoke Sunday morning feeling like shit, but a long soapy shower seemed to bring the aches under control. Like a good gay Eagle scout, I vowed to go to this gathering prepared: douche, grade papers, douche again, skip lunch—what doesn't go in won't need to come out, flush that thing one more time just for good measure, dress in clothing that can be easily discarded, pull a bag of cheese curls from the grocery bag on the counter and head out the door with the wrinkled strip of paper bearing Jamie's address in hand. Winding through the maze of streets that constituted his subdivision, I found his townhouse, an end unit in a conjoined row of six. Guest parking was inconveniently located two buildings away. Claiming a parking space, I lifted the cover on the console and transferred the bottle of lubricant to the patch pocket on my cargo shorts and exited the car.

Jamie answered the door barefoot and shirtless. "Come on in," he grinned as he stepped back to give me room to enter. I had always known from the clingy shirts he favored that Jamie's upper body was well defined, but seeing it bare made my mouth water. He was totally smooth with a deep bronze tan that highlighted the cut muscularity of his pecs and abdomen. A faint happy trail circled his navel and snaked down to disappear below the waistband of the gym shorts he was wearing. The shorts ended above the knee and showed off his toned and muscled thighs. His legs were as hairless as his chest and glowed golden brown. Stepping into his living room, I was surprised. The place looked like it had been decorated by an interior designer. A plush tan contemporary sectional sofa formed an L that defined the space, and solid wood book shelves covered most of one wall. Each shelf contained a handful of hardback books artfully arranged, framed photos in odd-numbered groupings, and a smattering of trophies, sculptures, and hand-thrown pottery. As Brad had indicated, one entire wall was devoted to an enormous HD television screen on which two college football teams were waging war. In the center of the space sat an oversized ottoman which matched the sofa. It seemed somewhat out of place in the room arrangement A solid wood end table which matched the wooden bookshelves sat at the of the sofa and bore bowls of chips and a square baking dish filled with what I assumed was Jamie's seven layer dip. A stack of maroon bath towels sat on the floor beneath the table. Carl was lounging diagonally at one end of the sofa, his legs dangling off the sofa's edge. He had on his customary t-shirt and gym shorts. A paper plate full of salsa, seven layer dip, and corn chips rested in his lap, and he was deeply immersed in the action on the screen. About two feet down from Carl sat Brad wearing a white wife beater and a pair of cargo shorts. He glanced up at me and grinned. "Great minds think alike," he said and indicated his shirt and shorts combo. I had tried on at least five different clothing combinations that morning before settling upon the black wife beater and khaki cargo shorts. Thank God I hadn't gone with a white shirt, or we would have looked like twins. Brad patted the sofa next to him. "Grab some food and join the party."

Jamie had closed the door and offered to take the bag of cheese curls and transfer them to a bowl. He pulled a can of beer from the plastic ring that bound the six pack and handed it to me. "I'll put the rest in the fridge," he explained. He disappeared into the adjoining kitchen, and I picked up a paper plate and began filling it with food. I plopped down on the sofa on the far side of Brad and balanced my plate on my knees. I opened my beer, took a sip, and then sat it on the floor by my feet, praying I would not forget it and knock it over on his solid wood floor. Jamie returned and picked up a plate of food sitting at the far end of the sofa and began munching on corn chips and dip. For a few minutes everyone just watched the game. I knew absolutely nothing about football, so I sat wordlessly and grunted agreement anytime one of them would comment on the action occurring on the screen.

About a half hour into the game, everyone had pretty well cleaned their plates and placed them on the sofa to their side. A player intercepted a ball and carried it almost all the way down the field before being felled. “Look at that!” Brad exclaiming, grabbing my knee and shaking it roughly.

“The man is fast,” I added, not knowing what else to say. Brad’s hand remained on my leg, and his fingers were softly stroking my skin. No one else seemed to notice, and I sure as hell did not mind. When the station cut to a commercial, Carl rose, stretched, and headed down the hallway to the bathroom. Less than two minutes later he returned looking smug and sat back down. He abandoned his reclining position, though, and sat on the edge of the sofa with his elbows resting on his knees, his chin cupped in his hands. When the game resumed, Carl leaned back and casually ran his hand inside the waistband of his gym shorts. He began stroking his cock beneath the flimsy nylon cloth of his shorts while sipping nonchalantly from the beer which occupied his other hand. A minute later, Jamie followed Carl’s lead and began massaging his package through his shorts. Brad’s hand began moving slowly up and down my leg, pushing the hem of my cargo short s further up my leg with each movement. So, it really was going to be this kind of party, I thought to myself.

By the next commercial break Carl had pushed the waist of his shorts down and his hard cock was in plain view as he continued to stroke it with slow even strokes. Jamie was still playing with his cock through the fabric of his shorts, but the tent his rigid member was creating left no doubt that he was willing to play this game. Brad had stopped playing with my leg and rammed his hand down inside the waistband of his cargo shorts and appeared to be kneading his cock as well. I could feel Carl’s gaze upon me, and when I looked in his direction, he motioned for me to come to him. I stood up and crossed in front of Brad. Carl released his cock and nodded toward it with his head. I sunk to my knees between his legs and lowered my face to his groin. Placing my right hand around the base of his shaft, I tilted the head towards me and began to tongue the tip. I ran my left hand up the leg of his shorts and began stroking his hairy thigh with my fingertips. I slowly moved up and down his shaft, taking more of his cock into my throat with each downward motion until his cock was buried in my throat. I felt Carl's hand upon my head, and he lifted his groin toward me to push my face into the fabric of his shorts and bury his shaft even deeper inside me. Holding my head down against him, he began to hump my face, slowly at first but then with increasing intensity. I could barely breathe, but I continued to suck as best I could, swirling my tongue along the underside of his cock as his shaft slid back and forth between my lips. Finally, he released his grip on my head. "Anybody else want some of this?" he intoned, like he was offering them some dip or another beer.

"I do," Brad responded. I pulled back, slowly releasing Carl's cock from my mouth. It shot upwards and slapped against his belly. I stood and moved down the sofa to where Brad was sitting. His shorts were unbuttoned and unzipped, and I was surprised to discover he was wearing no underwear beneath them. He had pushed them down mid-thigh, and as I approached he scooted his butt out toward the edge of the sofa to give me better access to his package. Kneeling before him, I grabbed his shorts and pulled them the rest of the way down his legs and over his shoes. I tossed them aside and ran my arms under his legs and hoisted them in the air. The look on Brad's face registered alarm, but he made no move to stop me. I lowered my face and nuzzled the inside of his thigh on his left leg, moving upwards toward his crotch as I licked and gently pulled the dense hair with my teeth. When I got to his cock, I rubbed my face over it and lifted it so that I could gain access to his hairy nut sac. Covering his left ball with my mouth I gently sucked it into my mouth and began to tongue it and roll it around on my tongue. Brad gasped and threw his head back against the sofa cushion. Releasing his left nut, I lavished the same attention on its partner. Brad moaned audibly. Slowly rolling his ball out of my mouth, I then turned my attention to his cock which was already dripping precum. I flicked my tongue across the tip to capture the sticky substance, then I pushed his cock upwards to expose the tender underside with its large vein bloated with semen waiting to spew. Starting just below the cock head, I flicked my tongue against the sensitive skin in a light teasing manner and worked my way down his shaft to his thick dark pubes. Then, in one continuous motion, I lapped my tongue upwards from base to tip and took the head into my mouth, rolling the tip of my tongue around the rim and sucking gently on the tip before plunging my face down to his pubes, his shaft entering my throat.

"Oh. My. God!" Brad exclaimed, his breath coming in gasps.

"Quiet over there. Some of us are watching the game!" Carl growled, but I could see from the corner of my eye that Carl was turned facing the show on the sofa and not the big screen TV, and his hand was still rhythmically stroking his own hard cock, the head of which still glistened from the attention I had just given him.

I continued working Brad's throbbing cock with my mouth and tongue, alternating between rapid , urgent sucking of his whole shaft and slower, more sensual attention paid to the head of his cock. Brad was raising his ass off of the sofa to meet my face, and his arms were planted on the sofa on each side of him to support his weight as he arched his back and moaned his appreciation of my efforts.

"Stop! Stop! I am gonna cum!"

I withdrew and his cock jerked back and forth of its own accord for a full minute before Brad's breathing returned to normal. I loved edging him, but this time I had almost taken it too far and brought him off before either one of us was ready.

"If you are finished over there . . ." Jamie purred in his best fake southern drawl. I glanced over at his end of the sofa and found him grinning widely. At some point he had pulled his cock out of his shorts and it stood, a sentinel waiting for a proper salute.

I did not even bother standing, just crawled on my knees to where his legs sprawled and took up residency between them. His cock was not as long or as thick as Carl's or Brad's, but it was nothing of which to be ashamed, that was for certain. I grasped his shaft in my right hand and lowered my face to his groin to repeat the performance I had just given to both Carl and Brad. Jamie moaned appreciatively as I took him in my mouth and began to tongue his hard member. I could not remember the last time I had sucked cock for this extended time frame, and my jaws were getting tired. Would I be able to chew solid food come morning? No pondering that possibility now, not with three hard cocks in need of servicing. Fortunately Jamie could not take very much attention to his cock before he was on the verge of spilling seed, so he gently but forcefully pushed my head from his lap and asked for a time out.

When I stood up from in front of Jamie and turned to return to my seat, I realized Carl had other plans. He had taken a bath towel out of the stack beneath the side table and spread it over the ottoman that had been positioned in the center of the room.

"Strip," he instructed. I pulled my clothes off and tossed them on the floor.

"On your back," he directed. He motioned for Brad and Jamie to join him. "Grab his legs," he commanded. I lay on the ottoman on my back as I had been ordered and pulled my legs up so my knees touched my chest. Jamie took my right leg by the ankle, and Brad secured the left ankle and they gently pulled my legs up until my hole was even with Carl's cock. Carl moved in closer, a bottle of lubricant in his right hand. He flipped the top open and drizzled lube onto my twitching hole, then used a finger on his left hand to work the oily substance into my anxious hole. He then squeezed some lube into the palm of his hand and slathered it on his waiting cock. Grasping his cock in his right hand, he used it to slap my ass a few times and then rubbed it up and down the cleft in my ass cheeks, teasing my hole by pushing against it, but failing to insert the head more than half way. When he tired of his foreplay, he aimed his battering ram against my sphincter and pushed hard. In one fluid motion he was embedded into my ass up to his pubes and his heavy nut sac slapped audibly against my skin. Leaning over me, he planted his hands on the ottoman on each side of my chest and began mercilessly pounding my ass with his rod. Pulling back until only the tip remained inside my sphincter, he slammed his dick to the hilt and then repeated the motion. He was not taking his time on this fuck; he obviously wanted to seed my ass and seed it now. Like a piston in a finely tuned machine, his cock slid in and out of my quivering ass. I had not been fucked this hard in a long time, and I knew the next day I would be so sore that I'd be shoving Preparation H up my ass for days. Within a few minutes, the intensity of Carl's expression changed and his eyes literally appeared to roll back in his head. With one final plunge, he buried his cock inside of me and I could actually feel the spurting semen as it flew from his cock. His entire body shuddered uncontrollably and I tensed and un-tensed my ass in an attempt to milk every drop from his cock. He stayed there, partially collapsed on top of me, his chest inches from mine and his face sweating from his performance. Then he slowly stood up and grinned. "Next," he said with a sly smirk. He raised his right hand and slapped Jamie's right hand in a high five. "We call this play 'tag team,'" he announced as he stepped back to make room for Jamie. Jamie and Brad had released my legs, and I lowered them for a moment to keep them from cramping.

"Roll over, red Rover," Jamie practically snarled, and I did as he directed. Jamie positioned himself behind me, and placing his hand on the center of my lower back, he directed me to squat a bit lower. I heard the top on the lubricant snap open and then the sound of someone stroking Jamie's cock to spread the lube from tip to base. Then his hands, sticky with lubricant, grasped my waist and I felt his cockhead slide into my ass. Jamie started with slow strokes, building gradually. I wondered if he would try to edge his cock in order to prolong the experience or if he would follow Carl's lead and give me a second "wham, bam, and thank you man" fuck.

From my vantage point, I could now view the television screen, and I noted the game was still in play—or at least some game was in play; I could not be sure it was the same two teams we had been watching earlier because I really had not paid attention to which teams were competing. Then Brad stepped between me and the television screen. I glanced up to see him grinning, his cock in his hand. He waved it back and forth in front of my face and asked seductively, "Want some?" In answer, I opened my mouth and he wasted no time stepping forward to slide his cock down my willing throat.

"Oh damn, that's hot!" Jamie exclaimed and his assault on my hole sped up significantly. Each thrust from Jamie's cock drove me forward onto Brad's dick, and soon there was an effortless rhythm established between the three of us. Suddenly Jamie was pounding my ass hard and fast. "Here it comes!" he yelled and his grasp on my waist tightened as his legs gave away beneath him and he collapsed to his knees. His cock had exited my hole so fast that his semen ran sloppily out of my ass and dripped on the towel below.

"Two outs. Bottom of the sixty-ninth. Ass is loaded," Carl proclaimed, slapping my left ass cheek for emphasis. "Time for a triple play."

Brad pulled his cock from my mouth and moved behind me.

"How do you want him?" Carl inquired.

Brad hesitated. "On his back," he finally said," I want to see his face while I fuck him." I shifted position and pulled my legs up in anticipation. My legs were tired. My jaws were tired. My ass, however, was still hungry for more. Damn, I chastised myself, I'm not just submissive; I really am a sex pig. "Drop your legs for awhile," Brad said, his voice much softer, less demanding than Carl and Jamie had been. To my surprise , he reached down and pulled my legs together and then straddled me . He bent over and balanced himself on his hands, placing them on either side of my chest. Leaning down to my chest, he licked my left nipple, licking in concentric circles around the aureole before lowering his lips to the now rock-hard nipple and gently nipping it with his teeth. He turned his attention to the other nipple and repeated the procedure. Then he buried his face in the thick fur of my chest and slid down my sternum, licking and gently pulling the hair with his teeth as he went. When he got to my navel, he dipped his tongue into its concavity and then traced my happy trail until my cock was bobbing under his chin.

"Hand me my beer," he directed, and Jamie reached over to retrieve it from the floor by the sofa. Brad straightened up and took a swig from the beer bottle, then tipped it slightly and poured in into my navel. Despite having been open for quite a while, the beer felt quite cold when it hit my skin. Brad smiled, then lowered his face to my navel and slurped the beer from my navel. He planted light kisses down the dark trail of hair leading to my groin, then raised his head and paused over my cock. For a second, I thought he was going to take my cock into his mouth, but then he shot upwards to a standing position. Jamie reached for my ankle to hoist my legs into the air, but Brad waved him away. "I got this," he assured them as he bent and ran his arms under my calves and lifted my legs in the air. Repositioning his hands on my heels, he pushed my legs up over my head, effectively rolling my ass up so he could position his cock at the now gaping sphincter and slide his rigid, dripping cock inside of me. He slid back and forth within me in smooth slow strokes, his eyes locked on mine. His tongue pushed through his lips ever so slightly like a kid concentrating while taking a test. "I want to plant my seed deep inside of you," he whispered to me as he leaned into me and began to pick up the pace. "You feel so good." His voice was husky and low, and there was something in his face I had not seen in the faces of the other men. They had been intent on garnering pleasure for themselves, but Brad was trying diligently to make me enjoy what was happening between us.

"Come on, Brad, give it to him like a man." Carl's voice was harsh and filled with disapproval.

Brad's face deepened in color and he began pushing harder, more urgently against me. I tightened my ass as much as I could and began to contract and release my rectal muscles to bring him maximum pleasure. The look on his face announced that my efforts were having the desired effect, and soon Brad was panting for breath as he buried his cock deeper and deeper inside my gut. Carl appeared beside of us, stroking his cock, which was once again rock hard. He bent his knees and aimed his cock between Brad's torso and mine and, two or three strokes later, shot a huge wad of cum onto my sternum. The sight of Carl's sperm hitting my chest was more than Brad could take and he dispatched his load into my ass. "Ahhhhhhhhh," Brad moaned as the waves of pleasure washed over him and his body stiffened and his back arched. Then, without warning, he collapsed on top of me, nearly knocking the breath out of me in the process. He lay there, his head beside of mine, his body sweaty and sticking to mine. Then, just as suddenly as he had fell on top of me, he jerked himself up off of me and took the towel that Jamie stood holding out to him. I slid off of the ottoman onto the floor and then slowly got up on my feet. Jamie thrust a towel toward me and I gladly took it and began mopping the sweat and lube and sperm from my body.

Looking around, I noticed Jamie had already pulled his shorts on, and Carl was in the process of redressing. Carl walked over behind me as I bent to pick up my jock strap and shorts from the floor. He stuck his hand into the cleft of my ass and submerged a finger into my hole. He pulled it out and held it under his nose. Grinning, he walked to Jamie and extended his hand under Jamie's nose. Jamie inhaled. "That is what the British call 'figgy pudding,'" and they both laughed. Brad retrieved my black wife beater from the sofa, and I slipped it over my head. The hair on my chest was still damp with the combination of sweat, lube, and Carl's cum, and my shirt stuck to it in places. One by one we filed to the bathroom to wash our hands, and Jamie retrieved cold drinks for each of us from the kitchen.

We settled back into our original places on the sofa. Feigning interest in the game, Jamie remarked to Carl, "Damn, you were right. That was better than pussy. Tighter, more intense. And the blow job was better than most women can give too."

"Would I lie to you about something like that?" Carl asked. "I told you that you wouldn't regret it." Turning to me, Carl added, "Jamie was afraid if he fucked you that would make him gay. I told him not to sweat it. I fucked the hell out of you the other day and then went home and gave another load to the old lady that night. The only difference between man pussy and regular pussy is that I don't have to worry about getting you knocked up."

I wasn't sure how to respond to that, so I didn't. I just sat there and pretended to be absorbed in the game. Don't get me wrong, I had had no delusions that Carl and I would somehow end up living together in a cottage with a white picket fence in some queer Norman Rockwell painting, but I didn't exactly enjoy feeling like I was nothing more than a cum dump either. Still, I reasoned, I had enjoyed the pleasure—and it had been intensely pleasurable—of three of the hottest male bodies in my faculty. There were more than a few of my coworkers—all female, of course—who would have gladly accepted the role of cum dump in order to be with just one of these men.

When the game finally came to a close, we all helped straighten up Jamie's living room and carried the leftover food and dirty paper plates into the kitchen. "Well, I don't know about you guys, but I sure as hell had fun," Carl said as we gathered our things to leave. "We should do this again sometime." The other two agreed with him. "In fact," Carl continued, "why don't we make this our reward for winning games? If the team wins on Friday night, then we have special entertainment at Sunday's party, but if the team loses, then we all have to abstain until the next win."

"Sounds good to me," Jamie readily agreed.

"I'm in," added Brad.

"Okay, it's settled, Carl declared.

I noticed I did not get a vote; it was just assumed the homo would want to be gangbanged on a weekly basis. Well fuck, they had me there because I did want to get humped by these hot bodies as often as possible.

Carl slapped my ass as we headed out the door and said prophetically, "Until next time." Carl had parked in Jamie's extra parking space, so he did not have far to walk. Brad, it seemed, had parked right beside of my car, so we walked in silence to the vehicles. I was unlocking my door, when he called over the roof of his car, "That was great. You are wonderful. Thank you." He blushed and averted his eyes, then swung open his car door and slipped inside. Waving seemed too effeminate, so I saluted him as he backed his car from the parking space and drove away.

At home, I showered and slipped into a pair of silky boxers. I loved the way they felt against my skin as I moved. I double checked my alarm and then went into the living room and plopped myself down on the couch to watch TV. Boozer, the beagle, curled up behind my knees and fell asleep with his head resting on my calf. My ass was sore, but I loved the way it felt so warm and still moist with their cum. "Boozer, you are sleeping with a slut," I informed him, but his head never stirred; he didn't seem to care.

CHAPTER FIVE

The next morning I awoke to the sound of a dump truck backing up outside of my house, or so I initially thought. Then the steady "beep, beep, beep," grew increasingly louder, and I realized my alarm clock was calling me from my bedroom upstairs. I tried to jump up from the couch, but my body was stiff and sore and felt like that imagined dump truck had succeeded in backing over me. I drug my carcass upstairs and disarmed the alarm, then stumbled into the shower and let the pounding hot water massage my aching muscles. Yeah, I thought, it's been awhile since I have spent that much time in some of those positions.

I made it to work in time to do my morning duty. Carl was already in place, holding up the wall and nursing a travel mug of coffee. He grinned and arched his eyebrows when we made eye contact across the span of tables crowded with yapping teenagers. Brad didn't show up until right before the bell, and then he approached me and not Carl. He appeared worried.

"Hey, would it be okay if I dropped by your room after school to talk for a few minutes?" he asked. His voice was serious and there was no trace of a grin or a smile.

"Sure. Anytime."

"Thanks. I'll see you then." The bell rang and he hurried off toward the gym.

All day long I wondered what Brad wanted to discuss. We were not close; we had never had a conversation that did not begin or end in sex. It was funny, though. I had initially lusted after Carl and wanted to feel him inside of me more than anything, but now I found myself drawn more to Brad than Carl. Brad was strikingly handsome with that mop of loose curls framing his angular face. His naturally dark olive skin tone had darkened even more after a summer of outdoor activities, and there was sincerity in his eyes and a softness in his voice that set him apart from the other men with whom I had spent the previous afternoon.

When the final bell rang to end the day, Brad was waiting outside my door. When the last student exited, he came in my room and closed the door behind him. I was sitting at my desk on the far side of the room, finishing grade entry on a test I had just given, so it took me a minute to save my work and turn my attention to Brad. Brad had taken the opportunity to posit himself on top of one of the student desks nearest my desk, his ass on the desktop, his feet in the seat. His hands were clasped tightly and his elbows rested on his knees.

"I was just wondering if I could ask you a few questions," he began, his face staring down at his feet. "They're kind of personal, and you don't have to answer if you don't want to. I'll understand."

"Go ahead. Shoot." Okay, so given the nature of our relationship thus far, maybe that wasn't the best word to use, but he didn't grin nor flinch, so I was in the clear.

"Does it hurt?" he asked.

"Does what hurt?"

"When we," he paused and his face reddened slightly, "When we enter you. Does it hurt?"

I could not believe we were having this conversation here, now, and I wondered what had prompted this question.

"At first," I said. I decided the honest approach was probably the best. He was asking for information, so why not give it to him? The serious tone of his voice and the total avoidance of eye contact told me this was somehow very important to him and that he was embarrassed just to be fielding these questions. I prayed to God no administrator or secretary was eavesdropping via the public address system. Our office staff was generally way too busy for anything like that, and there had never even been rumors of anyone being called to the office based upon such eavesdropping, so I felt relatively safe going into detail.

"At first it can hurt like hell depending on how thick the guy is and how much lube he's used. The wetter the better for the bottom. It takes a few moments for the muscles in my ass to realize what is happening and relax. Once I relax and get used to it, then it begins to feel really good. And after the first one, I am relaxed enough that I can totally enjoy whatever happens after that," I explained.

"What does it feel like to have another man inside of you like that?"

"Wonderful. I love the feel of a man inside me. I love the touch of his skin against mine and when he slaps against me on the down strokes, it feels like we are melding together. Plus, I really like bringing another man pleasure. I love knowing that he has enjoyed himself enough that he shot his load inside of me. Does that make any sense?" I asked. He still had not looked up, and I could not read his expression because that mop of dark curly hair completely hid his face when his head was hanging down like that.

"I guess so," he responded. "Do you do anything to get prepared for it?"

I laughed. "Yeah, no man wants to be a fudge packer. I use an enema syringe to flush out my rectum if I think I might get fucked that night. It is the gay man's equivalent of a douche. It can take five minutes, or it can take an hour. It all depends on the old GI tract."

We sat in silence for a few minutes, then he started to extricate himself from the desk. "Well, I guess that is all I needed to know. I'm sorry for asking you such personal questions, but I didn't know who else to ask." He started for the door and then stopped. He turned and asked, "Do you have a boyfriend?"

"Not anymore."

"Oh." He seemed on the verge of asking something else, thought better of it, and finished, "Well, thanks again for the info."

"No problem," I said to his retreating back.

After he had left the room and I could hear his footsteps grow faint as he traveled down the hallway, I began to pack up my brief case and head for home. It had been a strange day.

I did not see Brad again until Wednesday, and then he greeted me in the hallway with his usual smile and acted like nothing had ever happened. Whatever had been bothering him on Monday had apparently passed and he appeared to be back to his normal self. On Friday, I slipped a note into each of their mailboxes that said quite simply, "Win one for the wiener." The game was an away game, and I personally despise football, so I had to wait until the eleven o'clock news on Friday night to find out if the team had won the game. They had not. Since I was the entertainment, and there was to be no entertainment on Sunday due to the loss, I did not show up for the ritualistic boys-afternoon-out at Jamie's. Instead, I graded papers, cleaned the house, walked Boozer, and mowed the lawn one last time before draining the gas from the mower and wrapping it in a tarp for the winter. All in all, it was a damned productive weekend, but my body yearned to be filled with cock. I had not been entirely honest with Brad; I didn't just love the feel of a man moving inside of me, I craved it, needed it—it was how I tried to fill that empty void I felt inside.

Monday morning came all too quickly. Carl acknowledged me with a nod once I was in my customary place for morning cafeteria duty, my back leaning against the wall and my mind willing my cock not to get excited at the sight of Carl's hairy legs exposed in front of me. It had been over a week now since I had sex, not even to jerk off, and I found myself getting horned at the slightest sight of hot male skin. Brad did not show up for his usual morning conversation with Carl, but since he was not technically assigned morning duty, it was not like he was skipping anything.

Two more days passed in that manner before I found any relief. On Thursday morning Carl intentionally bumped into me as he passed while leaving the cafeteria and hoarsely whispered, "Later." When I opened my email during first block, I understood what he meant, and I could barely contain my anticipation. The email was short and cryptic: "Football office. Third period." Fortunately, I had to lecture almost nonstop for both blocks, so there was no time to think about what might happen when I got to the coaches office. When the bell rang at the end of second block, I nearly knocked students out of my way to get out the door. I headed to my station in our department's group office and retrieved the small brown paper bag I kept there for such emergencies. Always be prepared—what can I say, the lesson stuck. Hurrying to the men's faculty bathroom, I locked the door and turned the tap on the hot water. I let it run while I extracted an enema syringe from my bag, tested the temperature of the water with my hand, then filled the syringe and completed the task at hand. Boy was I going to be surprised—and disappointed—if I got to Carl's office and all he wanted was to discuss Jason's grades.

The door to Carl's office was open when I arrived. He was sitting behind his desk watching a video of last week's game on his computer screen. He was so intent on the image that he did not appear to notice me at the door, so I knocked and asked, "Is now okay?" Carl looked up and grinned.

"Now is perfect," he said. "I need a break from watching this shit or my blood pressure is going to spike. It continually amazes me how we can run the same damned plays every day in practice, and then on Friday night they can go out there and act like they have forgotten every damn bit of it."

"Not a good week, huh?"

"You can say that again. Then after the game that dumb ass Myers runs into my wife and tells her that the coaching staff has sworn to abstain from sex for the week after any loss. What the fuck was he thinking? You just don't say that to someone else's wife or girlfriend, damn it. Which explains why he can rarely keep one, the dumb fuck."

I wasn't sure what I was supposed to say to that, so I just sat down in the chair and said nothing. One of Carl's hands went instinctively to his lap. His cock was visibly enlarging under the flimsy nylon sweatpants he was wearing.

"At any rate," he continued, "she has made it her fucking mission to keep me from breaking what she perceives as my oath to the assistant coaches. It's been nearly a week now with no release, and I think my balls are going to explode if I don't shoot a load soon. I tried jerking last night, but every time I closed my eyes I saw your lips descending on my cock, and I just couldn't settle for a rough hand job." His hand had snaked inside the waist of his sweat pants and freed his cock from the jock strap that restrained it. He had pulled it upwards so that it was free from his clothing and it stood at attention pointing into his abdomen. "Would you?" he asked, his lips pouting and his face drawn into an expression of great sorrow. I could not help but laugh at this grown man acting like a little boy in order to get his dick drained. I had pushed the office door shut when I entered; now I got up and locked the door. When I turned back to face Carl, he had stood and his sweat pants and jockstrap were gone, having been swiftly shed and discarded in a pile on the floor.

I sank to my knees and took him into my mouth. Damn, it felt good to stroke his tender skin as I tongued the head of his cock. Reaching behind him, I planted one hand on each of his ass cheeks and squeezed as I slid down his shaft and took him deep into my throat.

"Oh damn! How I have missed that!" Carl exclaimed as I began a slow and steady rhythmic motion up and down his shaft, turning my head first to one side, then the other, to vary the pressure points being hit along the path. The vein on the underside of his cock was already engorged and I was pretty sure it was not going to take much to bring him off. Only a few minutes into this session, Carl pushed my head off of his cock and begged, "Can I seed you?"

My response was to stand and drop my own pants and thong. "No, leave that on," Carl directed," That is fucking hot. I've never seen a man wear one of those before." I pulled the thong back into place, and worked my pants legs over my shoes. Turning around, I bent over the arm of the love seat and spread my legs so Carl could position himself between them. He wasted no time. I heard him spit into his hand and then the head of his cock found its mark and he was inside of me, pounding hard and fast. He had no desire to make the moment last; what he wanted now was release, to dump a week's accumulation of cum deep inside of my willing gut, to feel his eyes roll back in his head and his legs become wobbly from the exertion of having every muscle in his body constrict at once to blow that load deep into the tight wetness that sucked at his cock with his stroke. The sound of his body slapping my ass was loud and filled the small room. His big balls slapped against mine on every down stroke, and his hands were kneading my waist roughly as he focused on one thing, and one thing only—giving himself the most intense pleasure he could milk from my body. Seconds later, he murmured, "I am coming!" and he drove his cock into my wet ass to the hilt and held it there as wave after wave of his seed spilled into my gut. It was so intense I could actually feel each spurt of hot steamy cum as it exited his now throbbing cock. I began to contract and release my ass muscles to milk him of every drop. I knew from past experience that he loved the feel of my ass sucking the last drops from his cock, and I wanted to make him feel as wonderful as I now felt. I knew Carl was only using me for his own pleasure, but how could I not be grateful to the man who was filling, if only temporarily, that void I felt inside? Carl stayed inside of me until his cock had gone soft, and then he pulled it out so slowly that I had to wonder if he were sad the experience was over so fast.

"That was phenomenal," came his voice from behind me. I could feel his semen running down the back of my legs. He slapped my ass playfully, and I pushed myself up to a standing position, still holding onto the arm of the love seat for balance. My legs felt as woozy as my head, and it took a moment for my equilibrium to return. I turned to face Carl, who continued to stand there buck naked from the waist down. His face held an expression I had never seen there before. "Your ass is fucking incredible," he whimpered. "That was the most powerful orgasm I have ever had in my life. Thank you. Thank you so much for letting me fuck you. I love my wife, I really do, but this is so much more intense." A pained expression crossed his visage as he realized what he had just said, and he covered his embarrassment by pretending to search for his clothes, which gave him an excuse to look at the floor and not at me. I pulled open his desk drawer and removed one of the hand towels that were waiting there. It was one thing to walk around the rest of the day with a smattering of his dried cum matted to my chest hair; it was quite a different story to walk around with this much cum running down my legs and my hole smacking from the wetness every step I took. Carl had located his pants and was pulling them into place. When his hands were free, I tossed him a hand towel and he wiped his crotch before sliding the jock strap and nylon sweats the rest of the way up his legs. I toweled my ass and legs, then looked down at the pouch of my thong and realized that it was soaked with my own cum. I had been so intent on feeling Carl's orgasm that I had not realized I was blowing my own load into the arm of the love seat.

I debated my options.I knew the string portion of the thong was sopping wet with Carl's cum in the back and the pouch was soaked with my own release in the front. I could leave it on and pray that it did not soak through my pants or I could remove the thong and go free balling the rest of the day. Both options involved risk of public humiliation, and there was no third option to simply put on dry underwear since I had not brought any with me. Maybe not so prepared after all. Hooking my thumbs under the skimpy cord that served as a waistband, I slid the soaked thong down my legs and stepped out of it before pulling on my slacks. The thong and the hand towel I had used lay on the floor at my feet. I started to retrieve them, but Carl intervened and scooped both of them up into his big hand and clenched them into a fist. "May I?" he asked with that arch of his eyebrows that made me go weak in the knees.

"If you want," I agreed, wondering what he was going to do with a cum-soaked thong. That was not exactly the kind of thing one hid in an office desk, especially an office where his assistant coaches may go rummaging and find it. And it certainly wasn't something one took home for the wife to discover. Carl grinned and raised the towel and thong to his nose and inhaled deeply. "Ummm" he moaned, "We smell so good together." He opened the bottom drawer on his desk and pushed the thong and towel into the back recess of the drawer, then slid it shut. He moved to the door and unlocked it, cracked it open and checked the hallway for any sign of Jamie or Brad, then pulled it wide open for me to exit. As I passed by him, his hand found my ass and gave it a squeeze. "So damn good," he whispered.

CHAPTER SIX

I was sitting at home watching TV that evening, enjoying the feeling of having had my ass opened up by Carl's large cock that morning, when the door bell rang. Boozer immediately started howling, and I had one hell of a time getting him to shut up. He had been sound asleep, and being startled like that immediately activated all of his protective beagle urges. I opened the front door to find Brad standing on the other side of the storm door, his hands rammed into his jeans and tears streaming down his face.

"Come inside," I said as I unlocked the storm door and pushed it open.

"I'm sorry to bother you, but I didn't know where else to go." Brad moved past me into the living room. "I'm just so confused, and I don't know what to do." The tears were streaming down his face, and he swiped at them with the back of his hand. His head was hung so that his hair blocked his eyes and I could tell he was embarrassed by his tears. Jocks don't cry, and all that bullshit.

"Sit down," I directed, "Make yourself comfortable." He sank onto one corner of my sofa and Boozer immediately joined him, hopping deftly onto the sofa and curling up next to Brad's thigh. Sensing Brad's emotional state, Boozer put his front paws on Brad's leg and rested his head on his paws. Brad immediately began stroking Boozer's head and long floppy ears with one hand, while the other hand alternately hid his eyes and swiped at the tears he could not will to stop flowing down his cheeks.

"Can I get you anything to drink? Tea, soda, beer, a glass of wine?" I offered while crossing to the small half bath tucked under the stairs. I retrieved a box of tissues and brought them back to Brad and placed them on the arm of the sofa beside of him.

"No, thanks. I'm fine."

My first instinct was to sit on the sofa beside him, wrap him in my arms and try to kiss away the hurt, but common sense over ruled that impulse and I took a seat in the big chair that sat nearest the end of the sofa where Brad was sitting. The chair was a remnant from my past life. It was a big square structure with wide flat armrests that made a good seat, and as a kid I had probably spent as much time sitting on the armrest as I had in the seat itself. When my parents replaced the living room set of which it was a part, I had drug it upstairs to my bedroom. Years later, when my parents decided to downsize, I had gone home to finish removing my junk from the old house and help transport their belongings to their new ranch style house. Unwilling to trash the old chair, I had lugged it home to my townhouse and paid to have it reupholstered to match my current décor. Boozer loved it as much as I did, and sometimes we battled for ownership.

I sank into the seat of the chair and pulled one leg up onto the cushion, then wrapped my arms around my knee. I waited as Brad slowly seemed to get a hold on his emotions. Petting Boozer seemed to be calming him down.

"What's wrong?" I asked.

"Everything," he sobbed, and for a moment I thought he was going to break down in sobs. "My life is so fucked up and I don't know what to do! I have tried to work through it by myself, but it is just not working. I've just got to talk to somebody, and I sure as hell can't talk to Carl about this, so that's why I came here."

"Talk to me."

"I don't know where to start," he whimpered.

"Well, let's start with whatever just happened that caused you to feel like you were losing control and brought you here," I suggested. Damn, all those classes in counseling and interpersonal communications were paying off.

Brad wiped away his tears and used a tissue to blow his nose. He crumpled the tissue and held it in his fist. "I don't know if you know it or not, but I'm engaged. We're supposed to get married next summer. So today after practice she had me meet her at the store to pick out the invitations, and then we went to the mall to look at china patterns and start gift registries. And the whole time we were there, all I wanted to do was cry. But I held it together until we got back to her apartment. She wanted me to come inside for awhile, but I claimed I did not feel well so I could escape." He paused and inhaled deeply. "As soon as I got back in the car and started out of her development, I started bawling like a baby and I just could not stop. I didn't want to go home. I share an apartment with a friend from college, and I couldn't let him see me like this. So I just drove around on the back roads for a couple of hours. And then I came here."

I waited, knowing my silence would prompt him to explore what was causing him so much pain. More than anything, he probably just needed to say aloud all of the thoughts he had been keeping locked inside of him for days, weeks.

"When I asked her to marry me, I thought I could go through with it." He wiped his eyes, but still avoided making eye contact with me. "I mean, it's what people do, you know? And she kept dropping all these hints that it was time. We couldn't pass a jewelry store without stopping to look at rings. And so I did what I thought I was supposed to do, and I thought it would make us both happy."

"But that's not what happened?"

He looked up at me for the first time. "That's kind of obvious, huh? I don't know what I expected, but it sure as hell was not this. I thought if we got married, then all of these feelings would just go away."

"What feelings?"

"You know what feelings. The feelings I have for men," he whispered. Good thing I was sitting down because I sure as hell hadn't seen that one coming!

"When did you start feeling that way?"

"I don't know. When did you?" he countered.

"I think on some level I always knew I was homosexual; I just didn't know what it was called. And when I did know, I knew society found it unacceptable, so I hid it from everyone, including myself, until I went away to college."

That seemed to give him confidence, and he launched into his own tale of discovery and denial. "I remember getting turned on by the sight of Bobby Marcus naked in the locker room in ninth grade. But then they told us that was normal; I mean, we teach that shit in health class now too, that it is normal for adolescents to go through a phase where they are attracted to someone of the same sex. So, I thought, okay, I'm normal. I just tried not to act on the feelings I had and kept hoping they would go away. And sometimes they did. And I started dating girls, and then one night when I took this girl home she told me her parents weren't home, and we went to her bedroom and we were making out and it got hard, and I creamed my underwear just fingering her. And it wasn't like I was imagining another man when it happened—I was totally into her, just her, and I came! So I thought, okay, that's proof that it was just a phase. But then the next day, I threw a boner when one of the guys slapped my ass as I was going into the showers after practice, and I felt so fucked up because the touch of his hand caused the same sensations that I had felt when I was with her." He stopped and raised his head to glance in my direction. "So that was the story of my life all through high school and college. Then I got the job here, and I guess I developed a crush on Carl. It was sick. I found myself hoping he would touch me. Slap me on the shoulder, punch me in the side, hell, even if his hand brushed mine while transferring paperwork, I was happy. But he was married and I knew he was straight, so there was no chance that he would ever think about me the way I thought about him. And that made it so much easier to control the feelings. I mean, it was a fantasy, you know, but an impossible fantasy, so I had this real life with Theresa and this fantasy life with Carl, and it didn't seem so bad." He pulled boozer all the way into his lap and cuddled him close to his torso. Boozer, eager to please, rolled slightly to expose his tummy, and Brad smiled slightly as he stroked Boozer's belly.

"And then . . ." I prompted.

"And then Carl started talking about having gotten a blow job from a guy once when he was drunk at a party in college. And he kept bringing it up any time we were alone together, saying it was the best blow job he had ever had, and how men were so much better at sucking cock than women were. So that day he asked me to go to the press box with him, I kind of thought he was going to ask me to suck his cock or maybe he was going to offer to suck mine. And then when we got to the top of the stairs, and you were there . . ."

"That must have been a major let-down." I finished for him.

"Yeah, it was." He looked up, and then scrambled to explain," No, I mean it was awesome—what you did was awesome, and I realized Carl was right. It is much more intense between two men." His gaze dropped to his lap and he focused intently on stoking Boozer's stomach. "But, yeah," he continued, "I was disappointed it was not me he wanted to do that with. That was the first time I had ever really seen his cock. Whenever we would be in the locker room or showers together, I would always look away from him because I was afraid he would see me staring and be repulsed by it. So to watch him stick that big cock into you and ride you like he did, My God , that was the hottest thing I had ever seen in my life. And I really wanted him to do that to me."

"So that is what prompted the visit to my room to play twenty questions?" I was beginning to get the picture now.

"Yeah, Seeing how much you seemed to enjoy taking him like that, well, I wanted to know what that felt like. I still do."

"So all that time you had reconciled your feelings for Carl by thinking it was an impossible dream. When you realized that Carl might return those feelings, is that what made you start questioning your relationship with Theresa?" I prodded.

"No. Carl is straight. He's just a sex addict, and his wife nearly caught him fucking some bimbo in the back of their van one night, so he started looking for ways to hook up with men. Because if he hangs out with guys, she won't suspect anything. But I know there is no future with Carl."

"So what has caused you to question your relationship with Theresa?"

He stared down at his hands, at the tissue he had been slowly shredding in his lap. "The sex," he said with embarrassment, "I had never had an orgasm as intense as the ones I had inside of you. And I started thinking, okay, I can just do what Carl's doing. I can have the wife and kids and the normal life at home, and still get fucked on the side, and maybe that will satisfy these urges that I feel all the damned time."

"But . . ."

"But that's not really fair to her, is it?"

He was starting to tear up again, and his voice choked with emotion. "I don't want to live a lie. If I marry her, I'll be lying to her . . . and to myself. And now I'm having those desires for another man, and he's not married, and he's not straight, and he's not afraid to be who he really is. And every time I am near him, I just want to devour him with my hands and my tongue. And the feelings are so strong that I don't know how much longer I can try to hold them inside. But I don't know if he feels anything at all for me. And if I break my engagement and then nothing happens with him, I'll be alone." He looked up at me and added, "And I am tired of feeling alone." His face contorted and he started crying again. He dropped his head and reverted to stroking boozer's head and ears. "I just don't know what to do any more."

I let him cry. Hell, sometimes we all just need a good cry to cleanse the soul. After a few minutes his sobs subsided and he appeared to be getting himself back under control.

"Well, I'm no therapist, but it sounds like you are trying to deal with two separate issues at one time, and maybe that's the problem. That's what is making you feel out of control," I offered.

"What do you mean?"

"One problem is your engagement to Theresa, and the other problem is how you feel for this man. You need to separate the two."

"I'm afraid," he admitted.

"What are you afraid of?"

"If I break off the engagement, she is going to want to know why. And I can't tell her the truth because I don't know what the truth is. So what if I break off my engagement, and then this guy rejects me, huh? Then I have nothing."

"You need to make a decision about the marriage first. It's

perfectly normal for someone who is facing a major commitment like this to feel trapped, to have second thoughts. You just need to figure out if you want to spend the rest of your life with this woman. Forget what you owe her for a minute; you owe it to yourself to be happy. The famous cliché from Shakespeare—'to thine own self be true.' You need to be true to yourself, Brad, and figure out what you want. Then when you know what you want, go for it. If it is a life with Theresa, then go for it. If it is a life with a man, go for that. Give yourself some time. You've got a lot to sort through."

"But he doesn't have a clue I feel this way about him. If I decide that I want a relationship with him, and not just sex but a relationship, how do I do that?"

"Simple. You just tell him."

"Yeah, right, and if he rejects me . . ."

"Then you'll get your heart broken, and you'll come over here and pet Boozer, and we'll talk about it until you see a light at the end of the tunnel."

He looked up at me with those beautiful eyes, and a trace of a grin spread across his red, tear-streaked face, "It's that simple, huh?"

"No. Nothing in life is simple. And certainly nothing in a relationship is simple. Not at the beginning, not in the middle, not in the end. We all get hurt, and we all hurt others. That's just the way it is. You can't go through your life trying not to cause other people pain all the time because it will just leave you in pain, and it will cause you to resent the very people you have been trying to protect. "

"When I asked if you had a boyfriend, you said 'not anymore.' What happened?" he asked with obvious hesitation. His head was still lowered but tilted so that his eyes peered from under those lush dark curls that fell forward to frame his handsome face. He had broached a subject I did not discuss with coworkers, with anyone for that matter.

But he had just finished pouring his guts out to me, and I knew that it had not been easy for him to do so—these were things he had kept bottled inside of him for years, and revelation, I knew, always comes with a price: it makes one feel vulnerable. There was something so innocent in his voice when he asked that I felt compelled to break my vow and let him inside the wall I had built around that part of my life.

"It was a long time ago," I said. "We met when we were in college. He was a theatre major and I was an English major, so naturally we ended up in many of the same classes. One thing led to another, and we ended up living together in an off-campus apartment for the last two years of college. By then we were both 'out' to most people, and everyone accepted us as a couple, which was the only thing a gay couple could be at that time. When I got a job offer in this school district, we moved here because it was close enough to the city that he could commute and look for theater work. And everything seemed to be going great. And then he got sick."

"AIDS?"

"Good guess, but no. Cancer. But when you are a gay man working as an actor, the moment you cough, everyone assumes you have HIV, and they run for cover like you have the plague. People we had known for years didn't even ask; they just assumed. And then they disappeared. A lawyer friend advised us to have the deed to the townhouse rewritten with only my name on the title, which proved to be a wise move, since the moment Borden died, his parents swooped in and tried to take everything. I couldn't stop them from taking his body, burying him back in that hick town he had hated and longed to escape. They told all of their friends and neighbors I was his college roommate, which was true as far as it went."

"I'm sorry," he said softly, still petting Boozer's head.

"Shit happens. You mourn, but you learn to move on too."

"You never found anyone else?" His intonation was puzzling,

part question, part plea.

"I never looked."

We sat in awkward silence for a few minutes. Finally, Brad stirred and tried to dislodge Boozer from his lap. "I guess I should be going," he said as he rose from the sofa. "We both have to work tomorrow."

I rose when he did and followed him to the door. "I'm glad you stopped by," I told him. "I'm glad you felt you could depend on me to be here for you."

He turned and hesitated, then his arms came up and enveloped me in a hug, pulling me tightly against him. He held me for a long time, and the feel of his body pressed against mine felt so natural, so good. His soft locks were pressed against the side of my face, and I had to restrain myself from nuzzling my face into his hair and kissing his neck. He was a man of contradictions—his body hard from continual exercise, his hair and skin soft and tender. He was so conflicted about his sexuality that I had no idea what this prolonged embrace meant to him. Was it the embrace of one friend by another who needed strength and was trying to draw that strength from the embrace? Was it the embrace of a man-child who craved to be held and told that everything would be okay? Was it the embrace of a man consumed by a passion he could not express to the object of that passion, so he was using me as a surrogate? I felt like shit because I was standing there enjoying his vulnerability, loving the feel of his body against mine, and becoming aroused—not by sexual desire but by a desire to hold him, stroke him, calm him, reassure him, protect him.

At last, he loosened his grip around my torso and turned toward the door. He pulled the door open, then turned back to me and said, "Thanks for listening to me. I had to tell someone. I just couldn't keep it inside anymore."

"Well, I'm glad it was me," I reassured him.

He smiled slightly. "I'm glad it's you too."

CHAPTER SEVEN

The next day was Friday, and I was sure as hell glad that it was. It had been a long week. Brad and Carl were already in the cafeteria when I arrived for morning duty. I stopped and said hello, then crossed the room to take my stand against the far wall. A few minutes later, Brad started across the room toward me. Damn, he was beautiful! How in the hell had I not noticed this man before Carl brought him to the press box? I mean, yeah, I had noticed him, but not really realized how hot he looked, and because there was never any reason for us to interact, I had never known how sensitive he could be.

"Hey there," Brad announced as he took a spot beside me and leaned back against the wall, only inches separating our bodies. He was wearing after shave and it smelled damned nice. Had he worn it before and I just hadn't noticed? He clasped his hands behind his back and then leaned back against them. "I really appreciate last night," he said, staring out across the tables.

"No problem," I said.

"You were right. I do need to deal with the one issue before the other one. Depending on my decision regarding the engagement, the second issue may no longer be an issue."

"Very true," I responded, shifting my position because the smell of his cologne and the proximity of his body were getting me aroused. Great, I thought, the man comes to you for moral support, and all you can think of is stripping his clothes off.

"When I got home I sat down and started making a list of all the pros and cons of the situation. I've got to figure out what I want from the future and what I am willing to give up." His voice was even; gone was the emotional upheaval of the night before. He was approaching the subject pragmatically this morning, enumerating pros and cons, running a cost/benefit analysis. I wasn't sure that approach would work, but I understood the desire, the need, to objectify the situation, to step back from it in order to see the big picture more clearly. I had done the same thing numerous times.

"This is not an easy decision for you. I wish there was something I could do to make it easier on you, but there isn't. This is one of those things you really have to do by yourself," I told him.

"I know," he responded, "But will you be there to pick up the pieces when I crash again?"

"Of course I will," I assured him. "You can drop by my place any time."

"You mean that?"

"Yes, very much so," I smiled. Regardless of his decision, I wanted to know Brad better.

"Where do you work out?" he asked, changing the subject.

"The gym across the street from the school. I usually pack my stuff and put it in the car in the morning and then just head there after work before going home. Why?" I asked.

"Oh, I was just thinking if you worked out later in the evening, we could hit the gym together sometime. It would be nice to have a workout partner. I hate lifting by myself." He sounded disappointed.

"What time do you usually hit the gym?"

"Depends. Sometimes I just use the training room here at the school after practice ends. Most of the time, though, I go home and eat dinner before heading back to the gym. So it is usually seven or eight before I get there. You're probably in bed by then, huh? Except when some crybaby shows up on your doorstep and keeps you up half the night," he responded

"Nah, I stay up until midnight at least. I've always been a night owl. Getting up in the morning sucks, but that's life. Sometimes I take a nap when I get home from work. And you were not being a crybaby. Don't put yourself down," I admonished him and slapped his thigh with my hand before I remembered where we were standing. "Oh shit," I whispered, "I'm sorry."

He laughed out loud and shifted his position on the wall, raising his left leg so his foot was propped back against the wall. "Don't sweat it. No one is going to misinterpret that.'

"And just how can you be so sure I didn't mean it as a come-on?" I teased. He smiled and made eye contact for the first time since we had been standing there.

"Because that's not your style. That's Carl's style. You would wait until we were alone. And even then you would show restraint."

"Oh really? And how do you know this?" I asked, curious to hear how he had pegged my reluctance to make the first move in flirtation.

"Well, you had your chance to put a move on me last night if you had wanted to, but you didn't. It's not how you operate," he explained.

"What kind of jerk would I have been to take advantage of you last night? You're right. That's not my style." Damn, all the time I had been getting a read on him last night, and he had been doing the same to me. Or had he analyzed the situation once he got home and started his list? Had he wanted me to make a move on him? Was that why he had come to me? Then it hit me, how the hell did he know where I lived? I had never told him; that was for sure. And he had never been to my place before. "Which reminds me, how did you know where I lived?" I asked, turning to face him.

"Internet," he grinned.

The bell rang and ended any chance I had to pursue the subject further.

The team lost the game that night, so there would be no "entertainment" at Sunday's meeting of the boys' club. The weekend was dedicated to winterizing my townhouse—closing storm windows, replacing old weather stripping, cleaning the flower gardens and hauling the bags of debris to the local landfill. So when Monday morning came around, I was at least well rested when I reported to work and headed to the cafeteria for duty. Carl was not there yet, so I took my position against the opposite wall and waited for Carl and Brad to show up for their ritualistic morning conversation. Only a few moments later Carl emerged from the athletic hallway, but instead of crossing to his spot, he came and stood next to me.

"We missed you on Sunday," he greeted me. "You know you are welcome to join us on Sundays even when the team loses."

"Thanks, but I had a crap load of work to do around my house to get ready for the winter," I explained.

"Brad didn't show up either. He texted me on Sunday morning and said he had some issues he had to handle that afternoon, then this morning a substitute showed up asking about Brad's schedule. According to the sub, Brad's going to be out for at least three days. I texted him to find out what is going on, but so far he hasn't responded. You have any idea what's up?" he asked, leaning back against the wall and sipping his coffee.

I was pretty sure Brad had not confided anything about his engagement nor his sexual preferences with Carl. I was actually surprised that Carl was asking me—what had led him to believe Brad and I were close enough that he would confide in me rather than Carl? This was clearly a fishing expedition, but was Carl just trying to find out details on Brad's situation or was he also probing to see if Brad and I had developed a bond that excluded him? Carl liked to be in charge, and that seemed to include directing the relationships between all of the members of this newly formed clique.

"I have no idea. I have not heard from him since Friday morning," I responded. Okay, so at least half of that statement was the truth. Then, to shift the subject, I observed, "So Sunday, it was just Jamie and you, huh?"

"Yeah," he sighed, "and that was pretty tense."

"How so?" I had never sensed any animosity between the two of them before.

"Jamie made a bad call and ran the wrong defensive play in the game on Friday night. Ultimately, it cost us the win. I don't think I was very subtle in pointing that fact out to him on the sidelines, and he has been more than a little pissed off at me since," he explained, taking another sip of his coffee. "So Sunday was awkward—lots of silence. I left as soon as the game ended."

"He'll get over it," I offered.

"Yeah, but he keeps shit locked up inside of him until it boils over," Carl observed.

The bell rang signaling the beginning of first period, and we both pushed ourselves off the wall and started for our respective wings of the building. Just before we parted, Carl asked, "Tomorrow good for you?"

"Sure," I grinned, feeling my cock start to swell at the thought of being bent over the love seat in Carl's office with his large cock penetrating me.

"Looking forward to it," Carl smiled slyly.

Otherwise, Monday was rather uneventful. Tuesday brought the expected trip down the athletic hall to the football office. Carl was sitting at his desk when I walked in the office.

"Lock the door," he directed.

When I turned around to face him, I realized he had been sitting at his desk with his pants shoved down, stroking his already lubed cock in anticipation of my arrival.

"Whoa, big boy! What if Jamie or another PE teacher had come in here? Better yet, your wife?"

"Got it covered," he said, sliding his chair back under the desk so that his nether regions were completely covered. "And if it were the wife," he said, "I would have given her the same greeting you got." His smile broadened and he rolled his chair back so his cock was in full view. "Well," he sneered, "What are you waiting for?"

I stripped and placed my clothes on the far arm of the love seat, then moved to his chair and took his cock in my hand and stroked it from base to tip in slow, steady movements. "Feels good," Carl purred, his eyes closed and his arms crossed behind his head to create a make-shift pillow. Carl had beautiful full lips and I longed to kiss them, but I was pretty sure that was against the rules. Carl had no desire for anything more than sexual satisfaction. He was not gay; he was not even bi; he was just a horny fucker whom I suspected was not getting the quantity of sex that his libido required. I also suspected that his wife, who seemed a bit prudish, probably was not willing to give him oral service and that after fifteen years of marriage Carl was finding their sexual encounters too routine. Carl loved sex and while he was willing to bend his heterosexuality card in order to satiate his desires, there was no way he was going to rip the card up and cross over to the other side. So there was no way he was going to kiss a man romantically or reciprocate a blow job. The one time his lips had met mine his intent had been purely self-fulfillment—he wanted to retrieve a taste of the load he had just deposited there. Carl was in love with his own sexuality, and I suspected that when he jerked off it was to an image of his own body.

Still, the man had a big dick and he knew how to use it. If he thought he was the only person getting pleasure out of these encounters, let him think that. I shared his enthusiasm for sex, and I knew I was using him for sexual gratification just like he was using me. Carl's dick was stiff and rock hard in my hand and it jerked slightly with every stroke of my hand. I did not want him to shoot off in my hand, damn it. I wanted more than that. So I stopped working his shaft and turned around and assumed the position with my hands braced against the arm of the love seat, legs spread in preparation for his entrance.

"So, you really want this big piece of meat, huh?" He moved into position behind me, using his knees to push my legs wider. He rubbed the tip of his cock down the cleft in my cheeks and found my hole quivering in anticipation. He eased the head inside of me and paused. Then he plunged his cock into me to the hilt with so much force that my hands were dislodged from the arm of the loveseat and I flew forward, my face and hands buried in the seat cushion, my cock rubbing the armrest, and my legs dangling mid-air on each side of Carl's muscled thighs. He grabbed my legs and held them tight to his sides as he began to pummel my ass with his huge throbbing cock.

"It won't take long today," he panted. "I'm hornier than hell and have been pulling on this thing for hours." His body slammed against my ass in deep, hard thrusts, each downward stroke causing an echo to reverberate in the small room as flesh hit flesh. My cock was responding to the fury of his thrusts and had grown hard beneath me. Each thrust of Carl's hips rubbed my swollen cock against the arm of the love seat, and while it felt wonderful now, I prayed it would not result in rug burn later. In record time, I felt a wave of orgasm pass through my body and my load spewed onto the love seat armrest. I gasped, and Carl increased his rhythm, his cock now slamming into me at rapid fire rate. Finally, he buried his cock deep inside of my ass, jerked my legs back to increase the depth of penetration, and convulsed as he shot load after load of his spunk deep inside of me.

For a long time, neither of us moved. His knees rested against the side of the loveseat to keep him from falling, his hands still gripped my legs and held them tight to his body. I could feel him panting for breath, and his cock was pulsing inside of me even as it began to soften. Finally, Carl withdrew his cock and released his grip on my legs. I heard the desk drawer slide open, and I knew he was retrieving a hand towel. I fumbled to right myself from my current position, feeling like a tortoise that has been flipped onto its back. I managed to get to my feet, but the process was not graceful.

"I needed that," Carl said, "I didn't just want that, I needed it." His eyes met mine and he added, "I'm sorry I couldn't hold out longer. Next time, I promise to take more time so you can get your money's worth too."

"That was hot," I grinned. "And I think I got my money's worth," I whispered, touching the arm of the loveseat that was soaked with my cum. Fortunately , it did not appear as wet as it felt.

"You shot?"

"Most definitely."

Carl reached out to touch the wet fabric and then sniffed his fingers. "Mmmmm," he intoned, "You sure did." He tossed me the hand towel. "You better clean it up this time. That was a six day load, so it is liable to flood down your legs if you don't."

We cleaned up and redressed in silence, then I wished him a

good day and opened the door to leave. Just as I was passing the door to the men's P.E. office, the door opened and Jamie Myers charged out.

"How goes it?" I asked as I kept walking past him.

"Fine, I guess," he responded, "considering we lost again."

He stormed down the hallway toward the football office, and I was damned glad Carl had made this a quick one. Jamie was already mad at Carl. Had he found the door locked, he would have unlocked it and come in to discover us fucking. I was pretty sure that would not have set too well with Jamie.

The rest of the day went quickly and soon I was back home, changing into more comfortable clothes. Stripped bare, I stepped in front of the full length mirror on the bedroom wall and lifted my cock to survey the damage. The skin was definitely red, but it did not burn or look too irritated, so I treated it to some shea butter and pulled on a loose pair of sweats. A slow walk around the neighborhood allowed Boozer to mark every tree, mailbox, and garbage can in sight. When he started lifting his leg but nothing came out, I figured it was time to go back home. "Looks like we are both drained for the night," I told him as I tugged his leash and headed toward the townhouse.

CHAPTER EIGHT

When I arrived at work the next day, there was an email awaiting me. Jamie had written: "Can I talk to you about something during planning period? We can meet in the P.E. office." Oh shit, I thought, he is trying to get me into the middle of this feud he has with Carl.

I decided not to mention Jamie's email to Carl while we stood together during cafeteria duty that morning. No need stirring in shit. Carl and I did not share much in common besides the fact that we both loved his cock up my ass, so there was not a lot we could chat about. He had again abandoned his post to stand with me on the other side of the cafeteria. Brad was out again, and we both seemed to be feeling his absence.

"Hear anything more from Brad?" I asked.

"Nope." Carl took another drag from his travel mug of coffee. "The little fucker is maintaining a code of silence. Maybe he's becoming a monk."

"Well, hopefully he'll be back tomorrow."

When the bell rang, we parted ways and headed to our respective areas of the building. For a Wednesday, the time seemed to pass quickly, and soon the bell rang ending second block. I was not really anxious to speak to Jamie, so I piddled around as long as possible before heading to the athletic hall. I did not like being put in the middle of two people—unless each of them had a cock in me. I definitely did not want to be asked to choose sides between two grown men having a pissing contest over a bad call during a damned football game.

Jamie was in the office when I arrived. He grabbed a computer disc from his station and said," I need to set everything up for practice after school today. We are watching last week's game before we hit the practice field." He opened the door and left the office. The implication was that I was to follow him, so I did. He headed toward the auditorium. Because he was in charge of setting up the videos for the team to view on the huge screen that lowered from just behind the curtain line on the stage, Jamie had keys to the facility. He unlocked one of the main auditorium doors and held it open for me to step inside. The room was pitch black and Jamie made no attempt to turn on the lights. Instead he crossed to the door that led up to the projection booth and unlocked it in the dark. The stairs to the projection booth were dimly lit, but at least there was enough light to see how to navigate them. The same dim lighting filled the projection booth. Jamie crossed to the computer and the window that overlooked the auditorium. He hit the power switch on the computer and inserted the DVD into the slot.

"So you and Carl have been doing he wild thing in the football office, huh?" he said angrily as he crossed to a toggle switch on the side wall. I was not sure what to answer, and indeed no answer seemed to be expected because he kept talking as he pushed the switch and I could see the video screen begin to lower from the stage ceiling.

"I found your thong in his desk drawer yesterday and there was a big wet spot on the arm of the loveseat, so I know damned well that's what the fuck you were doing down in his office yesterday morning," Jamie spat the words in my direction.

"He makes these rules that none of us can have sex for a week if the team loses, and then he breaks them. Of course, the rules don't apply to him. Nothing ever does. He's God and we're all just his little playthings." He crossed toward me and I instinctively backed up. I had never seen him this angry, and I still was not sure exactly why he wanted me to be there. He stopped a few feet in front of me and hooked his thumbs under the elastic waistband of his sweat pants.

"Well, if he doesn't have to follow the rules, neither do I," he proclaimed as he jerked his pants down and let them fall to the floor. His cock was already hard and it shot out straight and rigid from his body as soon as the jockstrap released its stranglehold. Reaching out he grabbed my shoulders and pushed down with more power than I had expected. I like being submissive, but there was something about his anger that frightened me. Still, I sank to my knees, willing to take his cock and accept his load if that would diffuse his anger. He pressed against me and his cock was poised inches from my lips. I tried to raise my arms to cup the cheeks of his ass in my hands as I opened my mouth to tongue his cock, but the grip he had on my shoulders did not allow much mobility. Just as my lips made contact with the head of his cock, he slammed his cock down my throat with enough force to tip me backwards and pinion me against the wall. His knees ground into my arms, pinning them to the wall, and he began to pump his cock into my throat with alarming roughness. With every thrust of his cock, my head slammed against the wall behind me. I tried to push him off of me, but my arms were pinned to the wall by his knees. He was frightening the hell out of me, and my fear caused my throat to constrict and I began to gag on his cock.

"What? Can't take a real man?" His words dripped with bitterness and were punctuated by an even more intense slam of his cock into my throat. I was having difficulty breathing and the constant slamming of my head against the wall was causing me to feel lightheaded. This was not a sexual encounter; this was an assault. If I got out this without a concussion I'd be lucky. A six day load had caused Carl to blast quickly yesterday; now I found myself praying Jamie would come quickly and this would end. My prayers went unanswered. Time seemed to stand still as he continued to bash my face into his pubes and the back of my head bounced against the cinderblock wall behind me.

"If Carl can have his little slut, then so can I. That fucker doesn't own everything," Jamie growled through clenched teeth as he continued pumping his cock deep into my throat.

"Bite him. Just bite him," a voice inside of my head kept screaming, but I was afraid to bite his cock for fear he would start beating me with his fists. He had me pinned to the wall with his knees and even if I scratched the hell out of his legs with my hands and clamped my teeth onto his cock, I knew he could still deliver a death blow to the side of my head with his fist before he let me go. This man was pure muscle and right now he had every strategic advantage of positioning. Relax your damn throat and survive, I told myself. Survive.

Finally, after what felt like hours, Jamie's body stiffened and a blast of hot cum shot from his dick and filled my mouth. I swallowed as best I could, but when he shot another load I knew it was leaking out of my mouth and running down my chin. He held his cock in my mouth as he began to soften. At some point, he had removed his left hand from my shoulder and grabbed my hair. He continued to hold my head back against the wall as he removed his cock and straightened himself, removing his knees from my arms. Finally releasing me, he stepped back and pulled his jock strap into place, then pulled his sweats up. I noticed the bottom edge of his t-shirt was wet with his cum where it had made contact with my face as he pumped his loads into me. He never said a word, just turned and opened the door to the stairwell and left. I slumped against the wall, closed my eyes, and listened to his footsteps as he descended the stairs, crossed the carpeted span of auditorium floor and then exited the main doors, the heavy door clanging shut behind him.

I looked at my watch in the dim light. Five minutes. The entire ordeal had lasted about five minutes, but it had felt like an hour. I pitched my torso forward so that I was on my hands and knees. My legs had been cramped into one position and were now tingling. I knew better than to try to stand just yet. When feeling returned to my legs, I managed to get up from the floor. Holding the wall I slowly made my way down the steps and into the darkness of the auditorium. The main doors were only a few feet away, but there was no way I could go out in the building like this. My entire face felt wet and the stickiness on my mouth, chin, and neck confirmed I was covered in cum. I touched the back of my head and it felt damp. Trying to remember the seating arrangement of the auditorium, I made my way down the side wall toward the stage. My eyes began to adjust to the darkness and I navigated the three steps up the side of the stage apron and onto the main stage floor. I found an opening in the curtains and worked my way around the myriad of set pieces that cluttered the wings of the stage to locate the dressing room doors. I prayed that one of them would be unlocked.

The door to the women's dressing room was locked, but when I pushed on the door to the men's room, it opened. I located the light switch and flipped it on. The space flooded with light and my eyes blinked in the brightness. I felt my way to one of the sinks in the counter that stretched beneath the mirrored wall. Bracing my hands on the counter, I surveyed the damage. My eyes were red and my face was wet with tears. I did not remember crying, but obviously I had. My chin was flecked with white globules of drying cum and a thick coating of saliva covered the area around my mouth and streaked down my neck. There were clear signs of petechial hemorrhaging around my lips. The bruising was common after rough oral sex, and I knew it would take days to fully dissipate. I touched the back of my head and looked at my finger tips—blood. Just great, I thought and suddenly wondered if there was a blood stain on the wall in the projection booth. I washed my face in the basin and dried it with the paper towels left sitting on a huge roll on the counter. I applied a wet paper towel with cold water to the back of my head and another one to my eyes. After a few minutes, I still looked like shit, but I no longer looked like a victim of a violent sexual assault.

I closed my eyes and just stood there trying to figure out what to do next. I had done nothing to deserve this. I owed Jamie nothing. Report it to my administration? I knew my administration. We would both be fired. Go to the school resource offer and report it as rape? I could hear his questions: Did you consent to go to the projection booth with him? Had you performed fellatio on him before? At any time during the incident did you tell him no? Somehow I could not picture myself telling this soon-to-be retired police officer that it was hard to say no to someone when they had a thick cock rammed into your mouth. Tell Carl? I knew Carl would respond by beating the living hell out of Jamie, and while I wanted that to happen, I wanted to be the one to do it. What I really wanted was Brad. I wanted to go tell Brad and have him envelope me in his strong arms and hold me and whisper in my ear that it would all be okay. But Brad was not here. He was off somewhere fighting his own demons. And I would have to fight mine.

I inhaled deeply and left the dressing room. Crossing the stage floor, I located the door to the hallway and left the auditorium. I was now in the performing arts hallway. I held my head up and walked down the corridor to the main foyer, then turned toward the athletic hallway. If that fucker thought he was going to get away with this, he was wrong. I had been scared, then hurt, but now I was mad, and with every step I became more livid.

I slowly turned the door knob to the men's P.E. office and then flung it open so that it crashed against the wall with a thud. Jamie was the only person in the room and he jumped up from his station at the sound. He was stronger than me, but this time I had the advantage—the element of surprise. I rushed across the narrow room and slammed him against the wall. He started to raise his arms in defense, but thought better of it and dropped them to his sides.

"Let's get one thing straight, you fucking rapist," I spat the words into his face and he flinched and closed his eyes. I slapped the side of his face hard and demanded, "Look at me when I'm talking to you!" He opened his eyes, but refused to make direct eye contact.

Instead, he seemed to be staring at some point beyond my head. I pressed my body tightly against his and gripped his chin in my right hand.

"I am NOT Carl's little slut. And I am not your little slut either. And I will not be treated like one. Not by you, not by anyone. Yes, I like to take the submissive role during sex, but that does not mean I am yours to use and abuse, you asshole!"

He was breathing hard and he had no choice but to make eye contact with me now because I was right in his face and my hand had his throat pinned to the wall. He could have pushed me away, but his arms remained at his side and his entire body appeared limp.

"I know you are pissed at Carl because he belittled you on the sidelines in front of the team on Friday night, but that is no reason for you to take your anger out on me." I shoved harder with my hand against his throat and he instinctively raised his arm to try to disengage my grip.

"If you EVER try anything like that with me again, I will bite your fucking cock off!" Jamie's face went stark white and his eyes widened. "I will chew that thing so badly with my teeth that by the time you get me off of you it will be too mangled for them to salvage it. Do you hear me?" he attempted to nod his head, but it was too tightly wedged against the wall. The most he could do was to dip his chin forward and back. Tears began streaming down his face.

"You want to know something, Jamie? You've spent years working on your body to try to make up for the way that doctor fucked up your face when he used those forceps to pull you screaming from your mother's body," I knew I was going too far, but I wanted to hurt him the way he had hurt me, "But what makes you repulsive isn't the outside of your head, it's the shit you have allowed to build up inside of it. Grow up, Jamie, and stop acting like a pathetic little boy who gets angry because he feels the other kids are excluding him. You raped me, you fucker! I should go to the office and report you." His eyes widened in terror, but he made no attempt to speak. "But I won't. I'll exact my own revenge."

With that I released my grip on his throat, and he slid slowly down the wall until he was sitting on his haunches, one hand grasping his neck and the other covering his face. I turned and walked from the office. Safe in the hallway, I exhaled and felt my hands start trembling. It took everything I could muster just to walk back to my room and collapse into the chair at my desk. I had only been in my room a few moments when the bell rang and students began meandering into the room. I took a deep breath and slowly exhaled it. Now, to finish the day.

CHAPTER NINE

That night I stood in the shower until the water ran cold, just letting the hot spray pound onto my shoulders and cascade down over my body. The anger was gone. In its place something hollow and empty had taken up residence. It was an all-too-familiar feeling—an old friend called numbness. After Borden had died, numbness seemed to fill me, and no matter what I did nothing completely erased it. His death had hurt much more than I had ever let show, and the way his family had treated me after his death still stung. So I had built a wall to protect myself from that kind of hurt. I was not stupid; I had taken enough psychology classes in college to recognize that the pursuit of no-strings-attached sexual encounters was nothing but a sad attempt to fill the void I felt inside. Still, the momentary elation at being one with another man's body, of feeling filled, was preferable to the risk of an emotional involvement. Sex was a cheap and inferior substitute for love, but it was better than nothing. It wiped away the numbness, if only for a little while. Feeling especially empty, I crawled into bed.

I awoke the next morning before the alarm clock sounded and turned to find the bed empty beside me. Well, with the exception of one overly-spoiled beagle who lay stretched out on his side snoring loudly and contentedly. I had dreamed that Brad had come into my room and crawled into the bed with me. He had snuggled close behind me and pulled me back against his body. The sensation had been so strong, so wonderful that I had awoken almost immediately.

I gazed out the window at the overcast sky that blanketed the area. Perfect, I thought, for a fucking Thursday. Would this damned week never end? I pulled myself from the bed and stumbled downstairs with boozer on my heels. He got a drink of water, and I opened the door for him to go take a dump in the back yard. I unwrapped a protein bar and ate it while he roamed the yard searching for the perfect spot. When he was finished, he sauntered back to the door and barked once to be let inside. We went back upstairs and he jumped on the bed and settled in for the day while I hit the shower.

Carl was waiting for me in the cafeteria when I finally arrived. I had wasted as much time as possible before reporting to duty because I really did not want to talk to anyone, especially Carl, and most especially Jamie.

"Did you hear the big news?" Carl asked as soon as my back hit the wall beside of him.

"No. What?"

"Brad broke off his engagement," he announced.

"Really?" I sighed, carefully controlling the intonation of my voice. "Guess that is what was bugging him then. Who told you?"

"He did," Carl replied. "He's here today. I think he is going through all of the notes the substitute left about his kids. Some of them were total assholes to the sub. I had to go intervene a couple times when we were in the gym."

The bell rang and we parted ways. The overcast sky outside seemed to have made its way into the school because my morning classes were very subdued. They barely talked and worked in silence on the reading assignment and accompanying worksheet I had given them.

When third period came, I sat down at my desk and began grading the worksheets that had been submitted that morning. The classroom door was open to the hallway and the noise from other classrooms with their doors ajar drifted into my room. I heard someone clear their throat and looked up to find Jamie Myers standing just inside of my doorway. I glared at him but made no move to get up or to speak.

"I know you don't want to see me," he said softly, "and I don't blame you. I wouldn't want to see me either. Hell, I never do want to see me. Nobody does."

"Sell the self-pity somewhere else. I have work to do and I'm not buying it."

He was quiet a second, then he reached out and closed the door.

"I fucked up."

"No shit, Sherlock!" the bitterness in my voice was not lost on him and I saw him flinch.

"You were right. I did take my anger for Carl out on you, and you did not deserve that. I do that a lot—hurt the people who are nice to me. My therapist says it is because I think they will forgive me."

"I wouldn't count on it."

"I'm sorry." He twisted his hands uncontrollably and for a second I saw a scared little boy standing across the room and not a fully grown man with a carved body and a caved face.

"You're sorry?" I stood from my chair and leaned against the end of the desk facing him, my legs crossed and my arms folded across my chest. "You pushed me against a wall, forced your cock down my throat, and beat my head into a wall, and you're sorry? That's supposed to make it okay? All's forgiven? What do you expect me to do, Jamie, drop down on my knees and offer to suck your cock as a sign of good faith?"

That hit him, and he dropped his chin to his chest as his face reddened.

"I can't undo what I've done. I know that. I'm just here to ask that you try to forgive me."

"What do you really want from me, Jamie? I've already told you I won't report it." I crossed the room until I was right in his face. "What is it that you want from me now?"

His lips were trembling and tears filled his eyes."I came here to beg you." His voice caught and he stopped. He inhaled deeply and continued, "not to tell Carl and Brad."

"And why should I agree to keep this secret from them?"

The tears were streaming down his face now, but he made no attempt to wipe them away. "Carl would kill me, and if he didn't beat the shit out of me first, he would see that I got fired. Administration loves him. One word from him and I'd be gone. And Brad would never speak to me again." He paused, the tears coming faster and harder, his breath gasping. "They are the only friends I have. I can't lose them. Then I'll have nobody."

Without warning he folded into the desk beside him, crossed his arms on the desktop, and lowered his head onto his arms. Sobs shook his body and he cried uncontrollably. I couldn't help it—I felt sorry for him. I knew his life had been a living hell, that he had honed his athletic skills to try to gain acceptance from the boys who picked on him in elementary and high school, that he had sculpted his body to gain acceptance from the girls who made fun of him and shunned him as he grew up. He had learned to absorb their emotional violence and hide it within himself, where he no doubt added to it by beating up on himself. He had learned to see everything as a personal affront because it usually was one. Carl had warned me that Jamie internalized everything until it exploded, but I had not seen the signs and never imagined the explosion would be directed at me. His left wrist was visible, and I recognized the scar tissue that marked his wrist. Not all of his wrath had been directed toward others. I reached out my hand and touched his shoulder. He flinched like I had hit him and pulled away from my touch. The sobs increased and he began pounding the top of the desk with his fists. I sat in the desk across from him and waited. My classroom door opened, and I looked up to see Brad entering the room. He saw Jamie and stopped in his tracks. I shook my head no, and Brad quietly closed the door, leaving Jamie and I alone in the room.

I sat there wondering how in the fuck I had managed to get myself in this position. This was more drama than I could handle. This shit was the reason I avoided the so-called gay scene—too many wounded warriors fighting for the title of "Most Fucked-Up Adolescence." Jamie's sobs began to subside, but he kept his head plastered to his arms.

"I won't tell Carl or Brad," I said softly. "But you've got to promise me you'll call your therapist and get an appointment for today or tomorrow because you've got to get help."

He sniffled and began wiping his eyes with the backs of his hands. "How can I ask you to forgive me when I can't forgive myself?"

"That's why you need to get help and soon. Like today. Take the rest of the day off. They can call a substitute. Go see your therapist—tell him it is an emergency because it is."

He started pulling himself up from the desk. I stepped between him and the door.

"Get help today, Jamie. Don't put it off until tomorrow. Or you may not make it until tomorrow."

His eyes met mine and the color once again drained from his face. "How did you know?"

"Kindred spirits and all that shit, I guess."

"I am so sorry I hurt you." His body language and intonation told me he was sincere. His face contorted, and he wiped at his eyes with both hands. "Oh my God, what have I become?" he whimpered. I did not want to do it because I was still very angry with this man, but I put my hands on his biceps and held them there for a moment to see if he would shrink away from me. He didn't, and I stepped closer and enfolded him in my arms.

"You need help, Jamie." He had collapsed against me, his head over my shoulder; his tears falling on the back of my shirt. "Please, go get help." After a moment, he broke the embrace and composed himself before opening the door and heading into the hallway.

"I'm gonna call him now," he said as he pulled the door shut behind him.

I slumped into my chair and stared at the screen on my laptop. My mother's words drifted back to me from a distant time, "Never pet a wounded animal. When they are hurt, they will attack you. They don't understand you are trying to help them. It's a defense mechanism. All they feel is their own pain."

"Men," I said to the ghosts in the room, "Even the straight ones are fucked up."

CHAPTER TEN

Somehow I managed to get through the rest of the day without any more drama. When the bell rang at the end of the day, Brad was waiting outside my door. As soon as the last student exited, he came inside the room and closed the door. Dear God, I thought, no more drama! I don't have the patience to play therapist again today.

"I'm glad I caught you."

"What's up?" I asked.

"Two things. First, I wanted to tell you that I broke off the engagement last night."

"I'm sure that was rough on both of you."

"Yeah, she did not take it too well. She kept asking me why, and all I could tell her was that I didn't think I could be the man she deserved to marry. I am not ready to 'out' myself to anyone, much less to her. She cried and screamed at me and I just sat there and took it. Finally she told me to get out, so I did. Her roommate was home, so I am sure they spent most of the night bashing me, which I deserve."

He rammed both hands into the pockets of his sweat pants with enough force that I was afraid they were going to slide off his hips and hit the floor. Not that I would have complained about the view, but I figured that was neither the time nor the place for that show.

"And second . . .?"

"Oh. What the hell was up with Jamie today?"

"What do you mean?"

"Oh yeah, right. Like I did not open this door and see him sitting here crying on your desk. And then as soon as he left your room he went to the P.E. office and made a phone call, and then he signed out and left for the rest of the day. So what the fuck is up? Don't tell me you don't know." He gave me his best attempt at a glare, but it failed miserably.

"I do know. But I can't tell you. I promised him that much," I replied. If anyone should understand my need to keep that confidence, it would be Brad. After all, I had kept his secret.

"Fair enough," he said as he planted his ass on the desktop across from me. "So what are you doing tonight?"

"The usual—gym, dinner, walk the dog, and grade papers. The excitement goes on and on," I snarled.

"Well, let's break the routine and go to the gym when I get out of football practice—about six. Wanna?"

"Sure," I grinned, "but you are driving because I am going straight home and fix myself a drink. I've earned it and I am going to have it."

"Rough day, huh?"

"You saw."

"Okay, got it. Well, I will pick you up at your place as soon as I can, but no later than six." He slid off of the desk and practically trotted to the door. "Catch ya later."

I finished packing my briefcase and headed for home. Boozer was elated to see me when I walked in the door. He raised his head up from the sofa and almost opened both eyes before returning to his slumber. "In my next life I want to be a dog," I announced to the empty house, "and not just treated like one."

I forced boozer off the sofa and into the back yard. Then I pulled down the bottle of vodka and a glass. Filling the glass nearly full of vodka, I reached into the fridge for the orange juice and added just enough to give the vodka some color. I let Boozer back in the house, and we both headed for the sofa. Mindless TV and a network news broadcast filled my time until it was nearly 5:30. I went upstairs and changed into sweats and a t-shirt, then grabbed a towel and a jacket, and headed back downstairs to wait for Brad. Ten minutes later, the door bell rang, and there stood Brad looking hot as hell and slightly flushed like he had been running.

"I got here as fast as I could," he explained as he stepped into the living room.

"You're not late, dude."

"Oh, okay." He flopped down onto the sofa and began stroking Boozer's ears.

I sat on the arm of the chair facing the sofa and watched him. When he glanced up, I asked "Are you okay?"

"Yes," he smiled, "Actually, I am. I thought I was going to be wracked with guilt and regret, but when I woke up this morning it was like a huge weight had been lifted off of me. For the first time in years, I felt free and almost comfortable in my own skin."

"Almost? " I laughed.

"Yeah, almost. This is all so new and scary, but at the same time exciting."

"Well, I don't mean to rush you," I said, getting up and heading towards the door, "but we need to hit the gym if we are going."

"Right." He pulled himself up from the sofa and headed toward the door. I held it open and he exited. I locked the door and turned to see him getting into a black Corvette convertible.

"Damn!" I exclaimed. "I had no idea we would be riding in this."

He grinned. "It's used. Trust me, I could not afford a new one."

"And here I thought they paid football coaches well."

"They do. But I'm only an assistant coach, and they only pay us enough to keep us off of public assistance."

We arrived at the gym in record time due to Brad's complete disregard for speed limits. Brad had brought a gym bag, so he headed to the locker room to store it, and I hit the weight machines. When Brad found me, he asked, "Don't you use free weights?"

"Not very often. Old back injury. Using the machines keeps my form correct and prevents injury. Sorry."

"No, that's cool. I've always used the free weight room, that's all. But I can give this a try. It's always a good idea to mix up the exercise routine so the muscles don't get used to what you are doing to them," he said as he adjusted the seat on the chest apparatus next to me.

The gym had the machines set up in a straight line, so that those of us who didn't really want to spend all day there but still wanted to get a balanced workout could just follow the line and complete a decent workout in about a half hour. Brad was clearly a workout junkie, so I doubted he would be very satisfied with this wussy set up that I followed. Still, he was a good sport and did not complain as we moved down the line of machines, completing three sets on each machine.

Then we hit the treadmills for half an hour and followed that by thirty minutes on the ellipticals. By the time we were finished, our t-shirts were soaked with sweat and plastered to our bodies. Sweat soaked the waistbands of our sweat pants and I was pretty sure we could both be smelled long before we were seen as we made our way to the locker room. Brad opened his locker and retrieved his bag.

"Why did you even bring that with you?"

"I brought a change of clothes. Usually I shower and change before heading home. That way if I need to stop at the store to pick up something for dinner, I won't be so gross."

"Makes sense. I'll wait out front for you if you want to shower before we leave," I offered.

He hesitated, then asked, "Can I grab a shower at your place?"

"Most certainly."

"I'll do that then," he said as he hefted the bag and headed for the door. The trip home was swift.

"Don't you teach driver's ed?" I asked when he slowed but did not stop for a stop sign.

"Yup. Sure do."

"So it's one of those 'do as I say, not as I do' things, huh?" I grinned.

"Something like that," he smirked as he whipped the car into the parking space in front of my townhouse. Boozer greeted us at the front door and immediately turned and headed to the back door. I took the hint and followed him to let him out into the back yard. I did not want to clean the kitchen floor that night. When I returned, Brad was sitting on the sofa with his gym bag on the floor at his feet.

"Come on, let's get you out of those soaking wet clothes." I started up the stairs. About halfway up the steps, I realized what I had said and hoped he did not misinterpret my meaning. Then again, what had I meant? Freud would be having a field day with this one, I thought. Brad had just broken his engagement; the last thing I wanted to do was pressure him into any kind of sexual activity or gay relationship. On the other hand, I could not deny the attraction I was developing for this man. I stopped in the upstairs hallway and pulled two bath towels from the closet and handed them to him.

"The bathroom is through the master bedroom," I said pointing to the door that opened off of the bedroom where we were standing.

"Aren't you going to shower?" he asked sheepishly. He had set his bag on the bed and was pulling out his street clothes and laying them on the foot of the bed.

"Of course, but you can go first."

"I tend to use a lot of hot water. You had better take your shower first. I can wait until you get out." He kept fiddling with his clothes and avoiding eye contact with me.

"Okay, if that works better for you," I said and began stripping the sweat-soaked clothes from my body and tossing them into the clothes basket that sat on the floor in the corner of the room.

Naked, I headed into the bathroom and started the shower. Once the water had warmed, I climbed into the tub, pulling the shower curtain closed behind me. After wetting my body down, I began to slather soap all over my body, enjoying the sensation of the hot water cascading down over my shoulders. I had left the bathroom door open so the mirrors would not all steam up, so I never heard Brad come into the room until he pulled back the curtain and stepped into the tub.

"Mind if I join you?" he asked. His eyes locked on mine and his smile spread mischievously across his handsome face. He didn't wait for an answer; instead he reached out and took the bar of soap from my hand and began sliding it across my chest and then down my sternum to my stomach.

"I'll stop if you want," he whispered hoarsely, the spray from the shower soaking his curly hair and dripping onto his shoulders.

"Don't stop." I reached out and cupped his face in my hands and drew him tightly against my body. Leaning in, I kissed him. His lips parted and his tongue snaked into my open mouth. He dropped the soap in the frantic embrace that ensued, and it is nothing short of a miracle that one of us did not step on it and send both of us crashing down. As the warm water poured over our bodies, our hands explored each other's body, stroking, caressing, and reading each other's reactions to every exploratory touch. Brad finally broke the kiss and began kissing my neck, my chest, slowly moving down my torso, tracing the treasure trail that led to his goal. With his left hand he lifted my cock and brought the head to his lips. Tentatively, he tongued the head before slowly engulfing it in his mouth. Slowly, very slowly, he began moving up and down the shaft, taking it a little deeper on every down stroke. He held his left hand around the base of my shaft and his right hand gripped the back of my thigh. The warm water continued to spray against us, and the sensation of the water pounding on my shoulders and Brad's attention to my cock was very rapidly bringing me close to orgasm. I was certain this was the first time he had ever taken a man's cock into his mouth. He was exploring new territory, and I felt honored that he had chosen me to be a part of his exploration of this part of his life, a part he had denied himself for so long. I did not, however, want him to choke on the explosion that was about to occur in his warm, wet mouth, so I ran my fingers through his sopping wet hair and gently pushed his head away from me. He looked up with an expression that said he feared he had done something wrong.

"You've got me too close to shooting. Are you sure you want to do that?"

In response, he returned his mouth to my rock hard member and began sucking hard and fast on my cock. Wrapping his arms around me, he grabbed my ass cheeks and pulled me in closer to him as he increased the rhythm of his strokes.

"Ohhhhhh," I moaned, "my God! Where did you learn to do that?" I cried as waves of pleasure coursed through my body and a huge load of cum shot into his mouth. Brad paused for only a moment before he resumed milking my cock with his tongue and throat. Another wave flooded my body and I was amazed he could take all of it on his first attempt at fellatio. Brad never stopped sucking my cock, and I was going crazy from the sensations emanating from my groin. A third explosion made me weak in the knees, and Brad slowed his pace and began softly tonguing my sensitive cock flesh as he pulled back and eventually allowed my cock to slip from his lips. Reaching up and grasping my hips for support, he stood and brought his lips to mine. Our mouths engaged and I realized he had held my spunk in his mouth the whole time. Now, as we kissed, I tasted my own seed as his tongue explored the inside of my mouth. Finally, when the water had lost all semblance of warmth, we shut off the water and stepped out of the shower.

Brad pulled a towel from the towel bar and began drying my body. When he had finished, I used the other towel to return the favor. Satisfied that we were reasonably clean and dry, Brad took my hand and led me from the bathroom into the bedroom. When he reached the edge of the bed, he dropped my hand and climbed on the bed and patted the space beside him. I followed his lead and lay in front of him, our bodies not quite touching as we lay on our sides face to face.

"I have to say I am amazed," I confided as I stroked his jaw line with my finger.

"By what?" he asked, a smile playing across his lips and a gleam in his eyes.

"Well, I certainly did not expect company in the shower, and I most certainly did not expect what happened next."

"I've wanted to do that to you for a long time. I almost did it the last time we were at Jamie's, but I chickened out because I did not want to out myself to Carl and Jamie. So, yeah, to be honest with you, we just fulfilled one of my fantasies," he paused, then laughed and added," And you played your part so well! I was sure you would insist I shower first, and then how in the hell was I going to justify joining you in the shower after that?"

"Ah-ha, so you played me, you devious stud."

"Kind of. Forgive me?" He mock pouted.

I ran my fingers through the damp curls that framed his face. "I'll think about it," I teased.

He began stroking the hair on my chest and then took one finger and made slow circles around the aureole. His touch was gentle and sensual, and my nipples both hardened in response to his teasing touch.

"Are your nipples sensitive?" he asked as his finger circled closer and closer to the nipple.

"Very," I gasped. His touch was driving me crazy

Scooting down a bit in the bed, Brad lowered his face to my chest and softly blew on the nipple he had been encircling with his finger. Then he grazed the tip of my nipple with the tip of his nose as he continued to gentle exhale upon the sensitive spot. Finally, his tongue flicked out and lapped at the tip of my nipple in rapid fire strokes that set me squirming on the bed. I rolled on my back to get away from his teasing tongue, but in a flash he was straddling my waist, his face lowered to the nipple, his tongue lapping the tip before he lowered his lips around the nipple and gently sucked it into his mouth. He lapped it with his tongue and then gently nipped at it with his teeth, sending me writhing beneath him. My cock had risen to full staff and bounced lightly against his backside as he straddled my waist and sucked first one nipple and then the other. I wove my fingers through his curly mop of hair and moaned my appreciation for the service he was performing on my chest.

"Someone seems to have risen to the occasion," he murmured as he paused sucking my nipple but kept his mouth poised over it, the gushing breath of his speech fanning the wetness he had just created. "Now, let's see how predictable you are," he added as he reached across the bed to pull open the nightstand drawer.

"Why, whatever do you mean, kind sir?" I intoned in my worst Southern Belle drawl.

"I mean," he said as he withdrew a large bottle of lubricant from the drawer, "That I was pretty sure you would have this stashed somewhere close by."

He sat upright, still straddling me, his knees pressed into the mattress on either side of my abdomen. Grinning like the Cheshire Cat, Brad made a big production of opening the bottle of lube and squeezing some of it onto the fingers of his right hand. I anticipated he would use it to jerk himself off and shoot his load all over my face and chest, so I was surprised when he reached behind himself and applied the lubricant to his own hole. More lube went into the palm of his hand and he reached behind himself again and grasped my cock and smeared it with lube.

"I've been practicing," he grinned, "With a butt plug that I ordered off of the internet, so I think I am ready for this. The question is 'Are YOU ready for this?'"

"I'm not a good top, stud. My cock shoots too quickly."

"Let me be the judge of that," he grinned as he lifted his ass and guided my rigid cock toward his hole. When he had the alignment right, he slowly eased himself down on my cock. I watched his face as the fat mushroom shaped head of my cock slid into his rectum. His eyes widened and a grimace contorted his face, but he didn't withdraw it. He paused, and I could feel his sphincter begin to relax its death grip on my cock. He inhaled and pushed steadily down until his ass touched my groin and my cock was totally embedded in his ass.

"You said it would hurt like hell at first," he gasped, "And you were sure as hell right!"

I pushed myself up onto my elbows to bring my face closer to his and leaned forward so that our lips found each other and I hungrily thrust my tongue into his mouth. For a moment we stayed in that position—him sitting on my pole and our tongues madly exploring each other's mouth. The kiss left us both gasping for breath, and a smile spread across his face.

"I think I've got it now," he grinned as he began to raise his ass off of my cock and then lower it again. "Oh fuck, that feels good—tight but good!" he moaned as his rhythm increased and he began thrusting his ass down on my cock with greater intensity.

I retrieved the bottle of lube from where he had dropped it beside us on the bed and poured some lube into the palm of my right hand. "Lean back some," I directed and he complied with my request.

"OH MY GOD!" he yelped as the movement had given my cock deeper penetration into his virgin ass. Grasping his cock with my lubed-up hand, I began to stroke him, trying to match the upward strokes on his cock with his downward strokes on my dick. "Oh Jesus!" he panted, "That feels incredible!" By now he was slamming his ass down on my cock with every thrust and the slapping of his ass against my groin created a cadence by which I stroked his cock. "You're going to make me come," he warned as he pounded his ass up and down my cock harder and faster .

"The feeling is mutual, "I whispered. "I'm getting close to

shooting . . .again. Damn man, the things you do to me!"

Sweat glistened on both of our bodies and we were both gasping for breath like marathon runners crossing the finish line.

"I . . .want . . .you . . .to breed . . .me," he gasped. "I'm gonna come. It's coming! It's coming ! Now!" he yelled as the first spurt of his cum flew out and landed on my chest. As the second load of his jizz erupted from his cock, I slammed my hips up to meet his downward thrust and my cock shot a huge load into his ass. He raised and lowered his ass a few more times to milk the last drops of cum from my cock. Then he collapsed on top of me and we lay entangled panting for breath. I wrapped my arms around him and pulled him tightly to my chest as we rolled to our sides and lay there nose to nose, eyes closed, a mixture of sweat and cum plastering us together.

"Now I understand why you love to bottom," he whispered. "That was awesome."

Once we had recovered, we hit the shower together and then headed downstairs to the sofa. Boozer was pissed that he had been outside for so long when he was certain something was happening inside the house. He wedged himself between Brad and me on the sofa and promptly fell asleep with Brad stroking his ears. We spent the evening holding hands and trying to hold each other—as much as that can be accomplished with a beagle wedged between two people. Unable to agree on what to watch on TV—he wanted the sports channels and I wanted a movie—we compromised on reruns of old TV sit-coms and true crime stories. When the late night news reports dominated the channels, Brad stretched and rose from the sofa.

"I guess I had better get going," he announced with a yawn.

"Why?"

"Because it is late. Because we both have to get up and be at work by 7:30 in the morning," he grinned and then added, "Because if I stay here any longer, I may not want to leave."

"Then don't."

"I think people would raise some serious eyebrows if I show up tomorrow in the same clothes that I wore today."

"You could wear a sweat suit of mine tomorrow. I have several that are clean and don't have holes in them or grass stains all over the knees. We're close enough in size that nobody is going to know that you are not wearing your own clothes. It's not like I have my initials monogrammed on them or anything."

"Are you serious?" The expression on his face had changed; gone was all trace of a smile, and I could tell that this moment was somehow a critical point for both of us. In the eleven years since my partner's death, I had never asked nor allowed another man to spend the night in my bed. It was one thing to have sex with them; it was another to wake up with them the next morning. Mornings meant bed-head and stale breath. Mornings meant lying in bed listening to the other person peeing in the toilet. Mornings meant awkward silence and even more awkward conversation over breakfast. Mornings meant commitment. And I had never wanted commitment. The pleasures of intercourse were immediate, intense, and fleeting, but so was the pain. I had known the pleasure of a committed relationship, but I had also felt the pain—still felt the pain—and now here I was staring at this beautiful, sensitive man whom I had just asked to spend the night without even giving it a second thought. The offer seemed so simple, but he was right, and I knew it: I was asking him to take this beyond casual sex where either of us could walk away without inflicting too much pain on the other one.

"Yeah," I said, reaching out and taking his hand and pulling him back down onto the sofa. "I'm serious. But I understand if you're not ready for that yet."

In response, he reached across my lap and retrieved the TV

remote. Aiming the remote at the cable box, he clicked the power button and the screen went dark.

"Let's go to bed," he said softly, a smile creeping across his face.

I let Boozer out in the backyard for his last chance to drain the vein, and then the three of us ascended the stairs and headed to my bedroom. Brad went through my collection of sweat suits and picked out one to wear the next day. I set the alarm half an hour earlier so I could fix a real breakfast instead of grabbing a protein bar. And then I crawled into my king sized bed and shut out the lights. That night I fell asleep with Boozer plastered up against my stomach and Brad spooning me from behind, his strong arm draped over my waist, his fingers interlaced with mine. I had just bought a ticket for the lottery; would I still feel as confident of winning when the morning sunlight streamed through my window?

CHAPTER ELEVEN

When the alarm clock blared the next morning, I literally bolted out of the bed to turn it off. I wanted nothing more than to fall back onto the bed and wrap my arms around Brad and go back to sleep. Somehow in the night Boozer had managed to wriggle between us, and when I turned and faced the bed, I saw him stretched alongside Brad, Boozer's head just under Brad's chin. Brad's eyes were open—well, slightly, and he started to push himself up on one elbow.

"Go back to sleep," I half-whispered, "I'll wake you up when I get out of the shower."

He didn't argue. His head hit the pillow and he wrapped his arm around Boozer and held him like a child would clutch a Teddy Bear. I hit the shower, roused Brad with a light kiss on the cheek, and then headed downstairs to fix breakfast. I love breakfast foods, but living alone I rarely took the time to prepare a real meal. Usually, it was a protein bar or a muffin from the coffee shop on the way to work. Surveying the fridge's contents, I realized how unprepared for this event I really was. We would be having eggs and sausage because that was all I had. Well, pancakes were a possibility, but I figured Brad had sworn off carbs. So I pulled a skillet from the cabinet and fried up some sausage, then drained the grease and crumbled the meat back into the skillet. Six large eggs joined the sausage and became scrambled eggs. I had just plated the eggs when I heard Boozer and Brad make their way down the stairs. Brad was already dressed for work.

"I gotta tell ya, it feels a little odd wearing your clothes," he announced as he dropped into a chair and picked up his fork.

"How come?"

He held up his hand with his pointer finger extended to signal one moment while he finished chewing the mouthful of eggs he had just forked into his mouth.

"I feel like I am wearing an advertisement that I slept here last night. Oh look, coach has on the English teacher's clothes! Wonder if they fucked last night?"

"Your students wouldn't dare! Or at least mine wouldn't. They would be too afraid of what I would do to their next set of essays." I paused for effect, then "Besides, it's not like anyone is going to notice the monogram on the collar," I added in a tone of dead seriousness.

Brad very nearly spewed eggs across the table as he frantically pulled at the collar of the sweat suit to see if there really was a monogram with my initials on it. Pulling the collar awry, he realized he had been played.

"You asshole!" he laughed as he readjusted the top and picked up his fork to resume eating.

"That's not what you said last night," I reminded him.

"And what did I say last night?" he smirked.

"Ahhhh! Ahhhhhhhh! OH MY GOD!!!!"

His face instantly turned bright red.

"You remember that, huh?" he asked sheepishly as he continued to fork food into his mouth.

"Yeah, it was the first time I was ever with a man who turned sex into a religious experience," I quipped as I began to devour my scrambled eggs.

"Are you always this punchy in the morning?" he asked, laughing.

"No, just when I have had incredible sex the night before."

He blushed again. Finishing the last of the eggs, he picked up the plate and silverware and took them to the sink, rinsed them, and then deposited them in the dishwasher.

"That was good," he said as he returned to his seat. "I've never had the sausage actually mixed into the eggs like that. Really, really good." He popped up from the chair. "You still need to get dressed, so I am going to take boozer for a short walk while you do that."

"Cool. Thank you."

"Not a problem," he said as he gathered the leash from the nail on the back of the pantry door. Boozer was instantly alert and came running to Brad. In fact, the two of them had bonded so quickly and Boozer had accepted Brad so unconditionally that I was beginning to wonder just whose dog he was.

I heard the front door close behind them, and I paused for a moment, fork literally suspended in air. How had this happened? And how had it happened so damned fast? Was it too fast? Were we rushing it and ultimately would kill it before it ever had a chance to develop into something real and solid? Shoveling the forkful of eggs into my mouth, I tried to dismiss my uncertainty. "You've got to stop using so many rhetorical questions," I reminded myself, "and you've got to stop talking to empty rooms!"

Duplicating Brad's actions, I rinsed the plate and deposited everything into the dishwasher. Then I headed upstairs and dressed for work. As I was tying my shoes, I heard the front door slam and the click-click of Boozer's toenails as he crossed the kitchen floor to get a drink from his water bowl. A moment later, an ESPN broadcaster's voice floated up the stairs from the television.

We left in separate cars, of course, but arrived in the school parking lot virtually at the same time. Go figure. Fortunately our assigned spaces were at opposite ends of the lot, so we entered through different doors and did not see each other again until we converged on the cafeteria. I was already at my post when Brad arrived and took up residence holding up the wall next to me. A few moments later Carl came from the direction of the main office; by his side was a young man in shirt and tie with a substitute lanyard hanging around his neck. Carl glanced in our direction, shrugged his shoulders, and continued down the athletic hallway.

"Wonder what that's about?" Brad pondered as he watched Carl and the substitute disappear down the hallway.

"Go find out, "I suggested.

"Nah, I don't want to appear too eager. Carl will tell me once first period starts."

Glancing at my watch, I informed him, "Well, you won't have to wait long then." A few seconds later the bell rang, and we headed our separate ways.

By the time I opened my school email, Carl had already sent me a message: "What the fuck is going on in this school this year? First Brad takes off for three days with no forewarning, and now Jamie has gone AWOL on the morning of a fucking game! I got called to the office this morning to guide his substitute through the first day because he has never subbed in P.E. before. According to the secretary, Jamie plans to be out all of next week!" A message from Brad basically relayed the same information, except it added, "But then you already knew this was going to happen, didn't you? Just saying."

The day passed quickly; well, it passed as quickly as a Friday can pass when you just want it to be the hell over so you can go home and nap. When the last bell rang and students streamed from my room, there was Brad striding across the floor like a man on a mission.

"Come to the game tonight!" he pleaded.

"Why?"

"Because I want you there. And with Jamie gone, that puts a hell of a lot more responsibility on me. And I want you there for moral support." He was practically begging now.

"Okay, I'll come," I said, like it was the most natural thing in the world for a man who hates football and doesn't understand the first thing about the game to attend an away game when he had never even attended a home game during the past fifteen years. Sure, I thought, I'll drive across town, pay God-knows how much to get in, and sit in the bleachers in the freezing cold just to see you walk nervously up and down the sideline yelling something I wouldn't comprehend even if I could hear what the hell you were saying. I would rather be at home getting ready for a one-on-one celebration or consolation party in my bed after the game, but what the hell. First one, then maybe the other.

"See ya after the game," and he was gone.

So I went home and let Boozer out to roam the back yard while I went through my closet and pulled out clothing for the night. I delayed leaving for the game until I absolutely had to do so, which meant I arrived after everyone else and there was no room in the stands. I took a position along the fence that separated the stadium area from the track where cheerleaders for the opposing team were chanting and assuming positions I had previously only seen in the Kama Sutra. Behind them the two teams were already engaged in the game. Our team was obviously lined up on the opposite side of the field. Well duh, dumbass, it was an away game, after all. I began moving around the fence, past the concession stand, toward the smaller and also totally filled bleachers on the opposite side of the field. A couple of students spoke as I made my way to a vacant spot along the fence. Well, if nothing else, at least from this vantage point I could watch Brad and Carl's asses as they stood on the sidelines and screamed at people. And that is basically what I did for the next two hours. Well, that and watch the scoreboard and cheer when everyone else on our side of the field sent up a cheer. We won the game by a slim margin, and Brad trotted over to the fence afterwards before heading into the locker room with the team.

"The team always goes to Godfrey's for burgers after a win. Want to come along?" He was smiling from ear to ear, and a part of me really wanted to say yes.

"That's going to make the players wonder why I am there, don't you think? Are you ready for that?"

His smile faded. "You're right. I'm not ready for that. See you at your place after Godfrey's?"

"Of course," I smiled.

It was nearly one o'clock in the morning before my door bell rang, and I was asleep on the sofa with Boozer. I stumbled to the door and opened it and Brad stepped inside.

"Your downstairs lights were still on," he stammered, "so I figured you were still up."

"I am . . .kinda," I slurred, glancing guiltily at the sofa. The arrangement of throw pillows clearly screamed that I had been asleep. I felt Brad's hands slide between my arms and my torso and clasp in front of my navel. His chin was on my shoulder, and the heat of his body pressing against my back felt wonderful.

"Let's just go to bed," he whispered near my ear, "and sleep."

"It's a deal," I murmured.

Taking my hand, he led me to the stairs and paused to flip the light switch on the living room lamps. Upstairs, we undressed and crawled into bed naked, snuggling together under the coolness of the sheet and the thin blanket. Lying chest to chest, our legs entwined, I ran my fingers through his hair, gently massaging his scalp, while he wrapped one arm over my waist and clutched my lower back. His other arm was tucked under the pillow. It was our second night together in my bed, and this time there had been no sex, but it still felt right.

I had turned off the alarm clock, so it was mid-morning before I awoke on Saturday. I rolled over, but there was nothing but an empty pillow there to greet me. Boozer had even deserted me. Damn, I thought, Brad's probably already gone. He had not mentioned any specific plans for the day, but it was not like we kept each other apprised of our daily schedules. We were not exactly dating, although we were spending a lot of time together since he had broken his engagement.

I drug my body out of the bed and headed to the master bathroom to shower and get dressed. If I did not go through the motions of getting ready to face the day as if it were a work day, I knew I would just lounge around the house all day like a hermit and then feel guilty come nightfall that I had accomplished jack-shit nada all day.

Emerging from the bathroom after my shower, I was hit with the most wonderful aroma wafting up the stairs. I pulled on a pair of old holey sweat pants and a threadbare t-shirt that should have been discarded a couple years before but I held onto it because it was just so damn soft and comfortable.

Boozer met me at the foot of the steps, tail wagging guiltily at having abandoned me in bed to follow Brad downstairs. I met the dog's big brown eyes and assured him, "I'd have followed him too." Boozer fell in behind me as I padded barefooted into the kitchen.

"And just who has been eating our porridge, Boozer?" I asked rhetorically as I approached the stovetop where Brad was busy maneuvering sausage links around a frying pan. I pressed my body against his back and ran my arms around his torso and squeezed him gently.

"I figured it was my turn to fix breakfast." He turned his head and I planted a quick kiss on his lips. "Now, sit down and wait for me to finish," he instructed, "it's almost ready."

Minutes later he carried a platter of sausage links, a small bowl filled with scrambled eggs, and a matching bowl filled with diced potatoes fried with green and red peppers and onions to the table. He had a carafe of orange juice chilling in a bowl of ice, and somehow he had found the cloth napkins I used once every ten years in the sideboard drawer and folded them into fans on the plates. I noted the silverware was in correct placement, and marveled that a jock would have this much knowledge of dining etiquette.

I reached to start filling my plate, but he playfully slapped my arm. "Wait for it," he grinned. He returned to the oven and pulled a plate covered with a dish towel out of its cavity, then twisted the control to the "off" position and approached the table. "The coup de gras," he announced as he placed the plate on the corner of the table and flipped back the hand towel to reveal a pile of steaming hot biscuits.

"You didn't . . ."

"Oh, but yes, I did. They are one hundred percent made from scratch this morning in this very room using these very rough but capable hands." He picked one up and lifted the top off of it to reveal that it had already been buttered. Picking up a bottle of honey from the center of the table, he drizzled honey over the steaming biscuit and then held it in front of my mouth. My eyes never leaving his, I took a bite from the biscuit, chewed it slowly as it virtually melted in my mouth, and moaned my appreciation for his creation.

"Delicious. Where did you learn to cook like that?"

"Only-child syndrome. My father worked in the city and was rarely home until late at night. My mother worked from nine to five every day, so I was taught to cook so I wouldn't starve. Today they call them latch-key kids. My parents called it self-sufficiency. When I was sixteen, I wanted a car. Dad said, 'get a job.' So I applied at the country club that was within walking distance of our house. I was hoping to be a caddy, but when they called me, they had different ideas. They needed people to help set up and break down the banquet facilities."

"That's where I learned this," he said taking the ornately folded napkin from my plate and flipping it open with a wave of his hand and arranging it across my lap.

"Did you get the car?"

"Damn right I did. It took me a year to save up the down payment, but once I had that, my mom agreed to co-sign so I could buy it in my own name and start building credit."

"Cool."

"I know one thing, earning that money made me value that car a lot more than if they had just given it to me. It was a used piece of shit, but it was MY piece of shit, and I felt like I had really earned the right to drive it. So many of the kids I teach get cars from their parents for their birthday, and it is not a used car or the family sedan being handed-down; it is a brand new sports car, and they don't appreciate it at all. They think they've somehow earned it just because they exist. They don't care if they wreck it; Daddy will just buy them another one.

That makes them really careless drivers."

"I'm sorry," he blushed, "I didn't mean to go off on a rant. Let's eat"

"You can rant to me anytime you want. I enjoy learning more about your life and what makes you tick." I reached across the table and stroked his forearm.

"Now eat!" he commanded, smiling. "I didn't slave over a hot stove all morning for you to let the meal get cold before you eat it!"

The food was delicious and the company very comfortable. It amazed me how easily we could just be in each other's presence without feeling the need to fill every moment with conversation. I had always hated dating someone for that very reason. The first date was usually pretty easy since neither of us knew much about the other one, so a steady stream of questions and revelation filled the space between us, but later dates often became awkward because the silence was tense with anticipation that someone should say something. It was easier to just have sex and send them packing, never to be seen or heard again. I stared at the handsome younger man sitting across the table. Why did this feel so right, so comfortable?

Brad caught me staring at him and asked, "What?"

"Nothing," I said, shoveling more food into my mouth, "Just wondering what I did to deserve this great meal with such a great guy."

He blushed. "It's the least I could do for keeping you up half the night waiting for me to show up."

"So what do you have planned for the day?"

"Well, I have to get my ass out of here and get to school by eleven o'clock to watch the tape of last night's game with the team. Pizza is scheduled to arrive at noon, then we will have practice until about two o'clock. After that, I have to clean my apartment, and then tonight I am going out with some guys from college. What about you?"

"Clean the house, do laundry, grade essays, drink, grade more essays, drink more, go to bed. That's the exciting weekend life of a typical English teacher," I moaned.

He laughed. "You should have learned to throw a football," he grinned, "then you could teach P.E. and not have to grade essays."

"Instead I would be attending practice...not a lot of difference. Neither of us gets to leave our jobs at the door when we leave that school building."

Brad helped clear the table before he grabbed his coat and left for school. I noticed he had packed a clean set of clothes in his gym bag the night before so that he would not show up this morning wearing the same clothes as last night.

The rest of the day drug by slowly, and I found myself glancing at the clock, hoping he would return that night. But when midnight came and went and still there was no Brad on my doorstep, I accepted my fate and went to bed alone. Boozer curled up against what had become Brad's pillow and fell asleep within seconds of hitting the bed. Sleep came much slower for me, and I found myself again pondering how I had come to feel so strongly for this man in such a short span of time. Was I setting myself up to get hurt? I had spent years building a wall to keep people out of my intimate space, never letting anyone stick around for long, never taking that risk. Why was I taking it now?

Sunday brought a text message from Brad: "Drank too much. Feel like shit. See you tomorrow if I live that long." Yeah, the age difference raised its ugly head. At least on Monday I would return to work with all of my papers graded and recorded and full lesson plans done. Damn, I was boring.

CHAPTER TWELVE

Monday morning Brad sidled up next to me as I leaned against the cafeteria wall and surveyed my kingdom of serfs eagerly eating their pop tarts and breakfast sandwiches while updating their friends on all the events of their weekend social life.

"Morning," he announced as he leaned back against the wall. "Sorry about yesterday."

I shot him a quizzical look and asked, "What do you have to be sorry about?"

"That I didn't come over."

"I had a crap load of work to do, so I would not have been much company for you," I lied, then added, "besides, it sounded like you were feeling a bit under the weather."

"That would be an understatement. I just wanted to sleep all day," he grinned, "so I did."

Carl joined us and the conversation quickly changed to Friday night's game, an appraisal of Saturday's practice session, and speculation about Jamie's whereabouts. Carl had tried repeatedly to call him, but all he got was voicemail options. He had even driven over to Jamie's place and Jamie's car was there, but no one answered the door when Carl rang the bell.

"Maybe it was a family emergency," I offered.

"Wouldn't he have taken his car?" Carl countered.

"Maybe he flew. If so, he may have had someone drive him to the airport or he could have taken the commuter bus. It is a hell of a lot cheaper than paying parking at the airport lot."

Carl seemed to accept that as a possibility. Why in the hell was I lying to provide cover for Jamie? I didn't even know for certain where Jamie was or what he was doing, but I suspected he was in therapy somewhere and just did not want to talk to anyone right now. He had a lot of demons to fight, and I understood his desire to be alone. Still, later that day I sent an email to his school email account: "Just let me know you are okay."

I did not get a reply to my email until Wednesday of that week. When I opened the email, I was torn. Jamie wanted to meet somewhere to talk. He suggested some place public like a bar or restaurant, someplace where "you'll feel safe." I didn't really want to talk about what had gone down between us, but I figured he may need to do just exactly that, and I wanted him to get his fecal matter organized and be able to live a healthy life, so I agreed to meet him at a local restaurant after school on Thursday.

I did not tell Brad about the email or the meeting because I had never told Brad about the encounter with Jamie in the projection room. And even though Brad and I were by no means a couple, he had spent two nights in my bed and we talked every day. I felt bad about keeping secrets from him.

Jamie was already at the restaurant when I arrived. The hostess pointed me toward a booth in the left corner of the restaurant. I noticed all of the other diners were seated on the right hand side, so we were totally alone.

"I taught Marla," Jamie explained, "so I asked if we could sit over here because we needed to talk about a student and confidentiality was needed to protect the kid's privacy."

I slid into the booth across from Jamie and waited. He had asked for this meeting, he could begin. He fumbled with the menu for awhile, casting furtive glances my way as I pretended to read a menu I knew by heart from all the take-out orders I had placed over the past year. Finally, he put the menu down and risked direct eye contact.

"Thank you for agreeing to see me." He hesitated. "I really didn't think you would." I looked up at him, but said nothing. "I know you probably hate me, and you have every right to," he paused. Was he waiting for me to object? "But your email gave me hope that maybe you can someday forgive me. You sure didn't hold anything back when you came into the office, and everything you said was true. I had been seeing a therapist for awhile, but I was not really making any progress because I didn't really want to admit some of the shit that I was feeling deep down inside of my gut. You kind of forced me to go there, and I hated what I saw. You're right—I was much uglier on the inside, and that's saying a hell of a lot."

I flinched and dropped my eyes. I had been especially cruel that day, and I had replayed the scene in my mind a thousand times, and each time I wanted to take back the hurtful words I had hurled at him. Making him hurt had not made me feel any less hurt myself; it had only compounded my feelings of betrayal with feelings of guilt.

"I'm trying to change that. I've been seeing my therapist every day since then. He made room in his schedule for me, but I could not get an after school appointment on a regular basis, so I just took the week off so I could focus on what I need to do. And it's working. At least I think it is. Just voicing some of the shit that I have carried around for so damn long has helped."

Our server approached the table and Jamie clammed up. He ordered an iced tea and I asked for a screwdriver. Jamie cocked an eyebrow. When the server left, he commented, "Need a stiff one to get through this, huh?" Less than a second passed before he realized the innuendo in his words and he blushed scarlet and hung his head."I'm sorry. I didn't mean it that way. Damn, I can't do anything right," he whispered hoarsely, his eyes clenched shut.

Reaching across the table, I laid my hand on top of his. He stiffened noticeably, but he did not withdraw his hand from under my touch. "I didn't take it that way," I offered. He opened his eyes and looked at me. "What happened, happened. Neither of us can take that day back and replay it to make it come out differently. I'm sure your therapist has told you that you cannot keep beating yourself up over it. I think we both know why it happened. Now we just need to get beyond that."

"I'm on meds now too," he said quietly. "It's hard not to hate someone when you've been hating them all of your life, especially when it's yourself."

"You'll get there," I said, trying to sound encouraging. I pulled my hand back as the server approached our booth and delivered our drinks.

Jamie ordered a plate of deep-fried mushrooms and a side order of ranch dressing. "Fuck the diet," he said smiling slightly. Maybe he was beginning to realize that six pack abs did not take away the pain inside.

"I'm coming back to work tomorrow. That's why I wanted to talk to you today. I wanted to warn you." He looked at me to see if there was a reaction. "My therapist wants me to get back into a normal routine. Apparently, he doesn't think hiding in my townhouse is a healthy alternative any more. I'm sure you know that Carl came looking for me."

"He's worried about you. So is Brad."

"I just needed to be alone for awhile." He sipped his tea. "But I can't keep hiding from the problem. I need to confront it head on, and that means returning to the scene of the crime. I don't know how I am going to go into that room again, knowing what I did to you there." His eyes filled with tears, and it pissed me off that I was feeling sorry for this man. "I know Carl is going to want to come over on Sunday afternoon if I go back to work tomorrow, and we both know what he is going to want to do."

"Yeah," I smirked, "He's probably getting pretty horned up by now."

"I'll understand if you do not want to come back to my place again. If you want, I'll refuse to hold it at my place; they can find someplace else to go."

I took a deep breath. "Listen, Jamie, I'm not going to pretend that nothing is wrong between us because it is, and it is going to take some time for me to get over it and trust you again. But, the bottom line is that I went to the projection room with you of my own free will and I did not exactly protest when it all started, so I have to own some of the responsibility for what happened there. I allowed myself to be put in that situation."

"You did nothing wrong," He insisted, "It was all me. Me and my anger at the world."

"And if you decide to host a party on Sunday afternoon, I'll be there."

"I promise I won't touch you."

"Yes, you will because if you don't touch me, Brad and Carl are going to know that there is something wrong and then they will start asking questions that right now neither of us want to answer."

He stared at the table top and swirled what remained of his tea in the glass. "I'll only touch you if you indicate you want it. Okay?"

"Deal. Now let's eat. I am freaking starving," I said as I noticed the server crossing the empty span of dining room with the heaping plate of deep-fried mushrooms. She slid the platter into the center of the table and cautioned us it was extremely hot, then lifted Jamie's glass and left to retrieve a refill.

"Damn, they never give me this many when I order them," I complained as I forked a few steaming mushrooms onto the small bread plate in front of me.

"The chef is a former player from a few years ago. I am sure the server told him who had placed the order. Coaching has its perks," and his face broke into the first unforced smile since we had sat down here nearly forty minutes earlier.

Some of the tension lifted as we each dove into the 'shrooms, alternating turns dipping the steaming morsels in the pot of dressing before savoring their slightly spicy goodness. Jamie seemed to relax some and his posture broke from its rigid and defensive former stance to become more at ease as the conversation turned from introspection to education and the ills of federal and state regulation in the guise of educational reforms. By the time the mushrooms had been depleted, Jamie seemed comfortable making direct eye contact with me, and I no longer felt the animosity I had harbored when I entered the restaurant. Jamie had fucked up—big time, but then so had I on numerous occasions in the past. We all fight our own demons, I thought to myself as I watched him savor the last of the mushrooms. And sometimes the demons win. We just had to keep on fighting.

Jamie picked up the tab, and I left the server a generous tip. Leaving the restaurant together, I had to admit to myself that the last half hour had been damned pleasant. I had often lusted after Jamie's body in the past, but now I had been given the chance to see the man who lived in fear behind that toned and trim façade. In the parking lot, we said our good-byes and headed to our respective cars.

When I pulled into my subdivision, I saw Brad's car sitting in front of my townhouse. I glanced at my watch. Practice would have ended nearly an hour before. Shit. Had he been sitting here waiting ever since then? I pulled into my parking space and shut off the engine. Climbing out of my car, I leaned on the hood and waited for the interrogation I felt sure was about to begin.

"Hope you don't mind I stopped by?" Brad asked as he exited his vehicle and crossed to my car. He crossed his arms on the top and mirrored my stance.

"Not at all," I grinned, still waiting for the real questions to start.

"So, are we going to stand out here all night," he licked his lips seductively, "or are you going to invite me inside and ravish me?"

Really? No "Where have you been?" or "What the fuck were you doing?" Was this man really NOT going to demand an explanation for my not being home when he arrived? A small voice in the back of my head sneered, "Jamie's not the only one fighting demons from the past, now is he?"

"Ravish you?" I asked in mock surprise and indignation as I stepped back and closed my car door and locked it. "Hell, no! That's your job—to ravish me."

Brad chuckled as he followed me up the walk to the front door. As I fumbled with the key in the door knob, his hands cupped my ass. "Can I get started right here, right now?" he whispered into my ear. His breath on my neck, his hands groping my ass, the slight brush of his chest against my back were causing a swelling sensation in my groin. It had been days since Brad and I had been intimate, and I was more than ready to strip his clothes off and make love to him in the foyer—if I could just get this damned key to work in the lock. Finally the key slipped into place, the latch moved, and we nearly tumbled into the townhouse as the door swung inward. Boozer hopped off of the sofa and trotted to the back door.

"Hold that thought," I told Brad as I bolted through the downstairs to open the back door and let Boozer go find a place to do his business. By the time I returned to the living room, Brad had collapsed onto the sofa, head and shoulders propped up on one end by throw pillows, feet dangling off the other end. I plopped down onto the floor at his feet and began unlacing his running shoes.

"You may not want to do that," Brad warned. "They get pretty rank."

"I'll take my chances," I replied, slipping his right shoe off and peeling the ankle sock from his foot. Contrary to his warning, his feet had almost no odor, due in part to the heavy dose of fabric deodorizer he habitually used on the interior of his shoes. Once I had both shoes on the floor and his socks draped across the toes of his shoes, I began to massage first one foot and then the other. He moaned his appreciation. I moved up his legs, massaging his calf muscles through the fabric of his sweat pants, then stroking his thighs, first the outer thigh and then the inner thighs, moving my hands along the muscles to stimulate the circulation of blood to the tissues below my fingers.

"That feels so good," he purred, trying too hard to sound lustful.

"You ain't seen nothing yet," I assured him as I crawled onto the sofa and lowered my body on top of his. He turned to his side and we settled into the narrow confines of the sofa, our legs entangled, arms wrapped around each other's torso. His lips closed over mine and his tongue snaked between my lips. His hips pushed against mine and I could feel the jab of his hard cock pressing against me. His tongue delved deep into my mouth and I felt a sudden desire to be one with this man, to meld with him so that our bodies were no longer separate but one being—like some deformed creature from the Greek myths, I thought fleetingly and wished that for once I could turn off my English-major brain.

Brad tried to shift our conjoined mass so that he would be on top of me, but the effort failed and sent both of us crashing over the edge of the sofa onto the floor. I hit the floor on my back with Brad on top of me. My head bounced on the solid wood flooring and for a moment I saw stars.

"Okay, that fucking hurt," I whined as Brad began disentangling himself from me and knelt beside of me, his hands on each side of my head.

"Are you okay?" His face was wreathed in concern, and his hands held my head steady against the floor.

"I think so," I said. "Why are you holding my head down?"

"In case you've hurt your neck."

"Brad, let me up. I am fine. Trust me, I have hit it harder than that before. I fell less than eighteen inches." He finally eased his grip on the sides of my head, and I began to struggle to an upright position.

Leaning back against the sofa, I took his hand in mine and joked, "Wouldn't that be a great story for the emergency room? 'And sir, how did you get a concussion?' ugh well, we were engaging in sexual intercourse on my sofa and rolled off onto the floor."

Brad laughed and squeezed my hand. "Don't joke about something like that."

"It's not the first time I've seen stars with you, but it is the first time it has happened when we've both still been dressed."

Brad pulled me to him and kissed me gently on the lips. Our prior kiss had been a kiss of lust, but this was a kiss of much more gentle nature. This kiss spoke words neither of us was ready to utter aloud. Brad stumbled to his feet and extended his hand to pull me up. "Come on," he whispered, "Let's take this show upstairs."

I followed Brad as he led me up the narrow stairs to the second floor and down the hall to my bedroom. Once inside the room, he turned and wrapped me in his arms, his lips nuzzling my neck and kissing me softly as he worked his way around my throat and up my chin to my lips. I pressed myself against him aggressively, wanting to feel his strength against me, opening my mouth to allow his tongue to snake inside. I sucked his tongue greedily and ran my fingers through his soft curly hair, gently massaging his scalp while keeping his face pinned to mine. Coming up for air, Brad grinned, "It's been awhile, but I had no idea you were this hungry."

"You know me well enough to know that I have an insatiable appetite for sex," I countered.

"I know this is about a hell of a lot more than just sex," he whispered, and his voice took on a serious tone that caught me off guard. "I want you, and not just your body, but all of you."

I cupped his face in my hands. "It's been a long time since I let anyone get behind the wall. It took a long time to build; it's going to take time to pull it down."

"But do you want to pull it down?"

"I want you. I want you more than I have wanted anyone or anything in a long time."

"Well," he grinned mischievously, "Here I am, take me."

He stepped back and began seductively slipping his shirt up his torso and over his head before letting it fall to the floor. His eyes never left mine as he hooked his fingers under the elastic waistband of his sweat pants and they dropped to the floor. He stood there in his boxers, his sweatpants around his ankles, grinning at me. I pushed one hand against his chest and he fell backwards onto the bed. I pulled his sweats off and tossed them onto the floor, then crawled onto the bed with him.

"You know," I said as I traced his jawbone with one finger, "I have not had time to prepare for this."

"That's not a problem," he grinned, "I did. Tonight you are on top."

In one swift move, he rolled over, pushed me onto my back and straddled me. He began slowly unbuttoning my dress shirt. He would loosen one button and then pull the shirt apart to expose more of my torso, then bend and kiss the newly exposed area before moving to the next button. When he reached my waist, he pulled the shirt from my slacks and opened it wide, then darted his tongue into my navel and began moving up my body, kissing and nuzzling until he reached my throat, then reversed direction and gently rubbed his face against my hairy torso as he returned to my waist. He loosened my belt and unzipped my slacks. My throbbing cock strained against my underwear and tented upwards through the open fly of my pants.

"I see you are up for the challenge," he said as he lowered his mouth onto my cock and began sucking it through the thin cloth of my knit boxers. He slipped his fingers under the elastic band and I raised my hips so he could pull my slacks and underwear down my thighs in one motion. He slid backwards off of the bed and removed my shoes, socks, slacks and underwear before returning to the bed to straddle my legs.

Brad lowered his body onto mine and began licking and sucking gently on first one nipple and then the other, causing me to writhe beneath him and moan my appreciation of his attention. Slowly he worked his way down my torso and nuzzled the inside of my thighs before lapping his tongue over my balls. Running his tongue up the underside of my cock until he reached the tip, he swirled his tongue around the head of my cock and slowly slid his wet, warm mouth down my shaft until he had taken the full length down his throat. He then began to move up and down on my rod, swirling his tongue and applying pressure to the tender underside on each upward stroke.

"You had better let up on that," I gasped, "unless you want a quick ending to this episode."

He released my cock and slid up my body so that my cock was now poised against ass cheeks. He bent down and gently kissed my lips. I thrust my tongue between his parted lips and explored his mouth while he ground his lips against mine. He began to lift his ass slightly and worked to position my cock against his tight hole. "Lube?" I asked breathlessly as we hungrily devoured each other.

"Taken care of that," he whispered hoarsely, "told ya I came prepared."

Bobbing his ass slightly against my cock head, he slowly pushed against me and I felt my cock slide inside his tight ass. Slowly he eased himself down on the shaft until he sat back and impaled my dick to the hilt inside of him.

"Oh baby," he moaned, "You feel so damn good inside of me."

I reached out and grabbed his waist as he began to ride my cock, slowly at first and then increasing in rhythm until the bed began to slam against the wall and I was certain the neighbors could hear his exclamations of pleasure.

"Fuck me, Oh yeah, baby, fuck me hard!" he begged.

I pulled him down against my chest, wrapped my arms around him and flipped him over so that he was now on the bottom with his legs wrapped around my waist. I grabbed his legs behind his knees and pushed them forward toward his head as I began to ram my cock into his tender ass with deep, rapid strokes.

He grabbed his rigid cock with his right hand and began stroking it in tandem with the pounding I was giving his ass. Our eyes were locked on each other and each thrust was an attempt to become a part of this beautiful man lying in my bed. Suddenly, he uttered a loud, guttural moan and his sticky white load shot from his cock and landed on his chest. The sight of his cum landing on his chest and chin was all it took to send me over the edge, and I slammed my cock deep inside of him and let the waves of pleasure overtake me as I flooded him with my load.

When my cock began to soften, I withdrew and lowered his legs to the bed. I collapsed on the bed beside him and pulled him on top of me. I loved the feel of his body weight pressing down upon me, the heaving of his chest as he breathed. I flicked my tongue across his chin to take the smattering of his load and then pulled his mouth to mine and we kissed for a long time before finally separating and lying side by side staring up at the ceiling.

"We better let Boozer in before we fall asleep here," he whispered.

He crawled off his side of the bed and headed into the bathroom to shower. I followed him, and we soaped each other up and stood beneath the cascading water kissing and exploring each other's body with soapy hands until the water began to grow cold.

I padded downstairs and let Boozer inside while Brad collapsed on the sofa in the living room and began flipping through the channels on cable searching for something we might both enjoy watching. Settling on a detective show, we settled onto the sofa with Boozer snuggled between us.

Sometime after midnight I awoke to find Brad and Boozer cuddled together fast asleep, the television broadcasting an infomercial, and my lower back wrenched in pain from sleeping on it in such a twisted state. I gently shook Brad awake, and he wordlessly rose from the sofa and headed upstairs and collapsed on my bed. By the time I shut off all the lights downstairs and made my way to the bedroom, Boozer had assumed a position snuggled against Brad's back. I set my alarm and crawled into the bed. For a long time I lay there staring at the back of Brad's head on the pillow, his firm, toned body covered by the flimsy sheet, my beagle snuggled against this man like he was a permanent fixture in my bed. How had this young Adonis broken through the wall I had so carefully built to protect me from falling for another man? Why did being with him feel as natural and effortless as breathing? I snuggled in closer to Boozer so I could wrap my arm across Brad's waist, and the three of us slept like one being until the alarm clock shattered the morning and announced another workday.

CHAPTER THIRTEEN

Brad had not been kidding when he said he had come prepared; the next morning he retrieved a fresh change of clothes from his car so he would not have to go back to his apartment or end up wearing my clothes to work. It was odd how we fell into a routine—I fixed breakfast while he showered; he walked the dog and took care of the morning dishes while I dressed for work. We left in separate cars, but arrived at school at the same time, entering through different doors and ultimately meeting again in the cafeteria where Carl and Jamie already stood conversing in low tones. I acted surprised to see Jamie back at work, and he repeated the same lame excuse for his absence that he had apparently been feeding Carl when Brad and I arrived. Talk quickly turned to coaching strategy for the upcoming game, so I drifted off to my assigned post on the opposite side of the cafeteria.

I found myself staring at Brad as the three chatted animatedly about the game. He was wearing a dress shirt and dress slacks since this was an away game, but the slacks were still tight enough to show off the firm bubble butt and those strong muscular thighs. Funny, only a few weeks ago my attention would have been on Carl's lean physique, but now the bond that was forming between Brad and I was changing my perspective on a lot of things.

The bell finally rang and the day officially began. Football players were especially antsy in class, and I felt like I was tap dancing just to keep their attention and try to get them through the period without losing all of the class to their unbridled energy. By lunchtime I was completely exhausted, and when the final bell eventually rang I locked the door to my classroom and race-walked to my car to join the throng of vehicles trying to get out of the parking lot.

At home, I let Boozer out for his afternoon ritual, then climbed the stairs, stripped, and collapsed onto the bed. Boozer joined me, choosing to rest his head on Brad's pillow. I snuggled close to him and inhaled the scent of Brad that lingered on the sheets and pillow case. I was not sure what cologne he wore, but it was light, fresh, and now it was associated totally with him in my mind. I awoke hours later when my cell phone rang, and it took awhile for me to get from the bed to my discarded slacks and extract the phone to answer it.

"Hey, we won!" Brad exclaimed as soon as I clicked the phone alive.

"That's great!" I responded, trying to infuse enthusiasm into my voice. In reality, I would have preferred they had lost. Winning meant a party on Sunday at Jamie's house; losing would have meant a weekend snuggling with Brad alone.

"You were asleep, weren't you?"

"You guessed it. Came home and crashed right after school. Which means I will be up most of the night now."

"Okay if I come over when we get back?"

"Sure. How long do you figure that will be?"

"I'll be there in about an hour."

"Okay. I'll order pizza. I haven't eaten yet, and I know you are always up for food after a game."

"You know me too well. Oops, gotta run. See ya soon." The line clicked and he was gone.

I drug myself to the bathroom and turned on the shower. A long, luxurious hot shower later, I was beginning to feel human again. Boozer and I went downstairs, and I let him out the back door to do his business while I located a menu from the nearest pizza shop and called in an order to be delivered in forty-five minutes. I let boozer back in the door and then walked to the front of the house to flip on the outside light for the pizza delivery guy. Grabbing the remote, I perched on the arm of the brown chair and flipped through the channels searching for something that might hold my attention without lulling me back to sleep before Brad or the pizza guy arrived.

Sitting on the arm of the chair mindlessly running through the channels, I pondered the conundrum into which I had thrust myself. I had promised Jamie that I would attend the party if such a party were held on Sunday, and at the time that had seemed like the right thing to do. But now I was not so sure. It had been a few weeks since the last group experience and my relationship with Brad had definitely deepened since then. I needed to broach the subject with Brad tonight and make sure that attending this party would not threaten what was evolving between us.

The pizza guy arrived first. I tipped him more than I should have, but having worked as a delivery boy back in the stone ages when I was in college, I understood how much those guys rely upon good tips to make ends meet. I had just popped the pizza box into the oven and turned it on warm when Brad opened the front door and announced his arrival.

"Mind if I grab a shower first?" he asked after an initial kiss. He had a gym bag in his hand, so I assumed he had brought a change of clothes. True, he had been coaching on the sidelines and not running the field with the players, but he had worked up a good sweat and I knew he was extremely self-conscious about body odors. He disappeared up the stairs, and I pulled the pizza out of the oven and set two plates on the table in preparation.

When Brad came back downstairs he was wearing a pair of pajama bottoms and a white wife beater. The white highlighted his olive complexion and clung to his body in a way that outlined every rippling muscle on his arms and torso. I was ready to ditch the pizza and attack him instead, but he dove into the pizza box with so much gusto that it was obvious sex took a back seat to pepperonis at the moment. Sliding three slices of pizza onto his plate, Brad pulled open the drawer by the sink and hauled out two forks. He handed one to me and then disappeared into the living room. I loaded my plate with pizza and joined him on the sofa.

He had switched the channel to a local station that was in the middle of a news broadcast. He sat cross-legged on the sofa with his plate balanced in his lap and carefully cut and speared pieces of pizza into his mouth as the sportscaster rattled on about the highlights of local high school games. Finally, the newsman came to the feature story—our high school's win over the defending district champion in tonight's match-up. Brad listened to the broadcast as though he were hearing the details of the game for the first time. As the sportscaster described the game, the station cut to coverage of several key plays and then a brief interview with Carl after the game. Cutting back to the anchor desk, the sportscaster announced that tonight's win cemented our team's position in the regional playoffs.

"Congratulations! That's a big deal!"

"You ain't shitting!" he exclaimed through a mouthful of pizza, "first time in four years that we have made the playoffs. Carl is hyped beyond belief." He wiped his mouth on a paper towel he had brought with him from the kitchen. "Oh, party at Jamie's house on Sunday. Needless to say, you are invited."

"Yeah. About that. We need to talk," I said as I put down the slab of pizza on which I had been munching.

Brad turned his attention from the television and lowered his fork with a square of pizza still attached. “What’s up?” he asked, his brow furrowing in concern.

“I don’t know if I should go to the celebration on Sunday.” I hesitated. I was not sure how to word this, but I was positive we needed to talk about it before any commitment was made.

“Why not?”

“Because you and I both know that Sunday’s celebration is going to turn into a sex party, and I don’t want to go if it might damage whatever is building between the two of us.”

Brad reached out and took my hand in his and gripped it tightly. “Okay, first of all, if you do not feel comfortable going, then you should not go. Second, don’t worry about anything that happens at those parties coming between you and me. The first time I really met you was at a party of sorts when Carl . . .um. . . brought us together, remember? So I am not going to go off like some half-cocked jealous boyfriend and get pissed about you having some fun.”

“So you would be cool with me being there?

Brad grinned. “Don’t take this the wrong way, but it really turns me on to watch you having sex with those guys. At first it turned me on because I wanted to be with you, and now it turns me on because I know that no matter how much they are enjoying the moment, I get to enjoy you for hours every other day of the week. Besides, Carl has plans for something new this week—something I think you would enjoy.”

“Really?” I asked seductively, “a new play for the playbook?”

Brad laughed and picked up his fork. “Yeah, something like that,” he said right before he stuffed a forkful of pizza into his mouth.

"Well, I guess I have to show up if the coach has a new play to test out."

"A new play and possibly a new player," Brad grinned, "Trust me, you're going to love this one!"

Try as I might, I could not get Brad to give me any clues to who or what might be in store for me on Sunday, but it was clear from his enthusiasm that he wanted me to attend the party. Once the pizza was gone, Brad pulled out the leash and he and I took Boozer for a late night jaunt around the neighborhood. The air was crisp, borderline cold, and Brad pulled me close to his side and wrapped one arm around me as we strolled with Boozer from tree to tree as he insisted on marking every possible landmark along the route. It was the first time Brad and I had shown any form of affection for each other in public; true, it was pitch dark and most normal people were in bed, but Brad made no motion to pull away when either of the two cars turned down the street and passed us.

Back inside the townhouse, we shut off the lights and climbed the stairs for bed. Somehow Brad convinced Boozer to sleep on the other side of him which allowed Brad to spoon behind me and hold me in his arms. It felt so right to have his arm around my waist, his torso pressed tight against my back, his legs entwined with mine. We were both sound asleep within seconds of hitting the bed.

When I awoke the next morning, Brad was gone. A note greeted me on the kitchen table telling me he had not wanted to wake me. He had let Boozer out for his morning constitutional before heading over to the school to watch the video of last night's game and the subsequent practice that would follow. By the time I had gone through my regular Saturday morning cleaning ritual and had a load of clothes in the washer, Brad was home. Well, Brad was at my house. I was in the kitchen when I heard the front door open and close. Then I heard Brad's imitation of Ricky Ricardo intone," Hey Lucy! I'm home!"

"You don't look Cuban, nor like a singer, but come on over here and I will check to see if you are wielding a tromboner."

He laughed as he crossed the kitchen, Boozer jumping excitedly against his legs. "I'm afraid not, but I do play a mean skin flute." He encircled me in his arms, and our lips met in a kiss.

"Good practice?"

"Great practice! Although Jamie had a sort-of melt down up in the projection booth. Not sure what the fuck that was about. When we got there, he did not have the tape set up and ready to go like he usually does. I mean, that's his job; he's always done that, but this morning he pushed the tape at me and asked if I wanted to do it this week. I told him I didn't know how to work the set-up up there, but he could show me. So we both went up and he showed me how to run everything. So once the film started playing, I left and came down to sit with Carl and the other assistant coaches. When the film was over, Jamie turned it off, but he did not come down with us like he usually does. The players pointed out what they had noticed from the game, and then Carl and the rest of us added some stuff to what they had mentioned, then we sent them out to the field for a short practice to loosen up their joints and keep them on their toes."

Brad paused and stared at me for a moment, then he continued, "Jamie still had not left the projection booth, so I went up to see what was keeping him. He was sitting on the floor, sobbing. I asked him what was wrong, but he wouldn't answer me. He just said he needed a minute to sort some shit out and for me to go on out to the field. So I did. He came out about a half hour later, red-eyed, but otherwise acting like nothing had happened." Brad paused again, then added," You know what this is all about, don't you?"

I nodded and averted my glance to the floor.

"But you promised him you wouldn't tell anyone, didn't you?"

"Yes, I did."

"Well, I'm not asking you to break that promise, but can you at least answer one question? Is he going to be okay?"

I looked him in the eye. "Yes, I think he is going to be okay. He has a lot of shit to work through, but I am pretty sure he is dealing with it as best he can at the moment. We all fight our own demons, you know. Sometimes we fight them publicly, but most of those battles have to happen one-on-one, just us and the demon."

"I understand. I really do. After all, it hasn't been that long since I was in his place—wrestling with my own issues, or demons as you call them." Brad smiled slightly. "And it feels so good to have won that battle and finally feel at peace with who I am and what I want out of my life."

I kissed him again. "Okay, the big question of the moment is . . . how are we each spending the rest of this day?"

"Well," Brad offered as he moved clothes from the washer to the dryer, "I have to return to my own abode and make an appearance so my roommate will not sublet my half of the apartment. I guess I should clean it as well since I am damned sure he has done nothing to it all week. He's being considered for a higher position in the company, and if he gets it, I may be looking for a new apartment or a new roommate."

"How come?"

"The new position would be at their corporate headquarters in Texas."

"So what about tonight? You have a hot date?"

"Well," Brad said, pulling me into his arms, "I was hoping to spend the evening in the company of a really hot man and his jealous beagle."

“I don’t know where you can find the hot man, but I have an idea where you can locate the beagle,” I smirked, looking down at Boozer sitting at Brad’s feet, his tail rhythmically thumping the floor.

Brad smacked my ass playfully. “You are the hot man—all the hot man I can handle or ever need.” His lips met mine and the heat rose between us as our tongues battled for dominance in this encounter.

Coming up for air, I asked, “Should we take this upstairs?”

“Nope,” Brad declared as he released me from his grasp, “I’m saving myself for tomorrow. ” He grinned wickedly and began backing out of the kitchen. “Tomorrow, tomorrow, I love ya tomorrow; you’re always a day away,” he sang as he sauntered across the living room to the front door.

“You’re a dick tease!” I shouted at him in mock irritation.

Opening the door, he turned and said, “I know. And you love it.” And then he was gone.

CHAPTER FOURTEEN

Saturday evening was spent watching movies on the television and taking Boozer for another long walk around the neighborhood before climbing the stairs for bed. Brad maintained his vow of chastity despite my repeated efforts to make him break it and met every attempt with the mantra, "Abstinence makes the cock grow harder," and an almost demonic grin. Boozer insisted on sleeping between us; it was a conspiracy, and I was not going to win this one.

Sunday morning Brad was like a kid in a candy store. He was so damned energetic and high spirited that I felt like kicking him. Whatever Carl had dreamed up for today's encounter, Brad was eagerly anticipating it, and I had to admit that the thought of once again having multiple men using my body for their sexual fulfillment was making me horny as hell. When it came time to leave for Jamie's place, I picked up my keys off the entry table and tossed Brad his keys.

"Why take two cars?" he asked, grinning, "After all, we are going to the same place."

"Okay, whose car should we take?" I asked, a bit surprised at this new development. While we had not exactly hidden our relationship from Carl and Jamie, we had not openly acknowledged it either. If we showed up in one car, the cat would definitely be out of the bag. Obviously, Brad was ready for that step.

"My car," he said as he took my keys from my hand and returned them to the tabletop.

"Can I bury my head in your lap while you drive?" I asked with a sneer.

"No, but you can as soon as we get inside Jamie's townhouse," Brad replied with a devious grin.

When we arrived at Jamie's place, Carl was already there. So was Jayden Laurence. Jayden was an assistant football coach, but he was not a member of the P.E. department. Instead, he taught math, so his classroom was one hallway beyond mine in the layout of the building. Jayden and I frequently ran into each other in the hallways as we moved from our departmental offices to our rooms. I had long admired his beautiful resonant voice. When Jayden opened his mouth, James Earl Jones seemed to speak. Jayden was about five feet, ten inches tall and built like a brick shit house.

Unlike Brad, Carl, and Jamie who each had broad shoulders that tapered to a narrow waist, Jayden's torso was straight and solid. At first glance, he appeared stocky, but a second look revealed a body that was pure muscle. His chest was well developed and belly was washboard flat. Thick, muscled thighs supported a deliciously appealing bubble butt. His mother was Caucasian and his father was African American, giving Jayden a beautifully rich caramel skin tone and soft curly hair that he now wore closely cropped to his scalp. When he had first started teaching at the high school, Jayden had worn his hair in a multitude of three to four inch dreadlocks, but after his first child was born, he had shorn the dreads off and resorted to a more sleek cut. It seems his baby girl had found his dreads mesmerizing, and Jayden had discovered how much pain a toddler could inflict by grabbing hold of a dreadlock and refusing to let go. So the dreads went and the baby stayed.

I knew from faculty gossip that Jayden and his wife were expecting their second baby sometime in early spring. While I had often wondered what was concealed beneath Jayden's habitual dress shirt and slacks, I had to admit he was the last member of the faculty I would have expected to show up at this celebration. Had Carl prepared him for what was undoubtedly going to happen here? Based on the devious smirk on Carl's face when I first noticed Jayden's presence, I was pretty damned sure Jayden had been prepped for today's party. If there was any doubt about the expectations of the event, the placement of the ottoman in the center of the room and the bottle of lubricant sitting beside it should have provided pretty strong clues.

The first half hour was totally social—grabbing beers from the refrigerator and feasting on crab dip and barbequed wings. The four coaches relived moments from Friday's football game, and I pretended I knew what the hell they were talking about. As the appointed hour for the pro game approached, everyone settled into their accustomed position on the sofa to watch the game. Carl was at one end of the sofa, Jamie in the middle, and Jayden at the other end. Brad and I took up residence on the shorter "L" portion of the sectional. The end of each quarter of the game meant a restocking of plates from the spread laid out on the kitchen table and another beer from the fridge. By the middle of the third quarter, it was fairly clear this was not an equal match and the outcome was relatively predictable.

Carl slid his hand inside of his sweat pants and began stroking his cock. Taking their cue from the head coach, Jamie and Brad did likewise. Jayden seemed embarrassed by their actions and stared intently at the screen. If that was causing him discomfort, I thought, he was going to flip out at what was coming next. Within a few minutes Carl had slid his sweats down to free his cock and it bobbed happily in the air as he stroked it nonchalantly with his right hand while holding his beer in his left hand and providing running commentary on the game. Soon Brad and Jamie had followed suit, although I noticed Jamie always waited for Brad to make a move before Jamie followed his lead. Jayden continued to stare at the screen like the secret to world peace was being revealed there. He made furtive glances at the other coaches when responding to some comment or question they had raised, but other than some squirming and adjusting of his crotch area, Jayden was not playing follow the leader.

Finally, Carl beckoned me to, "Come over here and take care of this," and I dropped to my knees between his spread legs and began sucking his cock. After a few minutes, Brad stood and moved to my side. When Carl pushed against my forehead with the palm of his hand, I released his cock and turned to take Brad's cock in my mouth. Jamie cleared his throat, which was my signal to switch. I released Brad's cock and repositioned myself between Jamie's legs. I flicked my tongue across the tip of his cock and licked up and down the underside of his shaft before slipping the head inside my mouth and beginning a full assault on his dick. Out of the corner of my eye, I could see Jayden press his left hand down on his crotch. There was no way he could not see what was happening on the sofa right beside him as fewer than four inches separated him from Jamie's thigh, and my head was planted between Jamie's legs while Jamie moaned loudly and appreciatively. I suspected this was the first attention Jamie's cock had received since he took off from work to concentrate on his therapy, so I tried not to arouse him too much too soon.

It's getting hot in here," Carl announced as he stood and peeled off his sweat shirt and sweat pants. Jamie bucked his hips upward and I grabbed his pants and pulled them down to the floor, my mouth still servicing his rigid cock. Brad's hands found the bottom of my sweatshirt and began tugging it upwards. I had to release Jamie's cock to finish pulling the shirt off over my head, and while I did that Brad pulled my sweat pants down. I toed off my running shoes and stepped out of the pile of sweatpants crumpled around my ankles. Carl was positioned at the end of the ottoman with the bottle of lube in his hand. I moved to the ottoman and sat on the edge facing Carl, then leaned back and pulled my knees up to my chest. Carl grabbed my hips and pulled me slightly toward him, then poured some lube into his hand and applied it to my ass. His middle finger stroked my hole and then slid slowly inside massaging the lube into my waiting ass. He poured more lube in his hand and stroked his cock to cover it with the sticky gel.

"The goal posts are set," Carl grinned, "It's time for a field goal!" Spreading his legs to achieve the right level for entry, he guided his cock to the opening of my hole and slid inside of me in one smooth stroke. Jamie stood on my right side, stroking his cock over me, and Brad stood to my left, working his cock over my chest. Carl handed the bottle of lube to Brad, who used some to wet his cock before passing the bottle to Jamie who did likewise.

"Ready, boys?" Carl asked with a full smile. He did not wait for a reply but began slowly fucking my tight ass with long slow strokes. On each downward thrust he ground his cock deep inside my ass and his balls slapped against my ass crack. Jamie and Brad were stroking their cocks at a faster speed than Carl was thrusting in my ass, but I was beginning to get a clear picture of the new "play" he had devised. As Brad and Jamie beat harder and faster on their cocks, Carl began to increase the rhythm of his cock inside my ass.

"Getting close," Jamie groaned, and Carl began slamming his cock deep inside of me. Within seconds, Jamie's cock exploded, sending huge globs of cum arching out over my chest and landing on my throat and nipples.

Seeing Jamie's load hit my body sent Brad over the edge and he began gasping for breath as he slammed his fist up and down his hard cock. Letting out an inarticulate yell, Brad shot his load all over my lower abdomen, and his cum pooled in my navel.

Carl was now pumping his cock into my hole in wild abandon. Then in one swift motion he pulled his cock out and aimed it at my face. A hot sticky stream of cum shot out of his slit and nailed me in the mouth. He continued to milk his cock and a second, smaller load fell between my pecs. I extended my tongue and licked his cum from my lips. He leaned his knees against the ottoman and bent over me. With one finger, he slowly swirled his way across my chest and down my torso, effectively mixing the semen spilt by all three men into one sticky finger painting on my torso. I lowered my feet to the floor and Carl extended his hands to help pull me to a standing position.

"You haven't come yet," Carl whispered. "And we cannot have that."

He turned me around, and I thought he was going to bend me over and fuck me again, but instead he wrapped one arm around my torso to hold me upright and then rubbed the other hand over my chest and abdomen until it was slick with cum, then he took my throbbing cock in his cum-lubed hand and began to jerk me off. It did not take many strokes before I was ready to blow a huge load.

"Catch it," Carl directed Brad. Brad moved beside of me and cupped his hand in front of my cock just as cum spurted forth into his palm. Brad then slathered my chest and abs with his hand, mixing my cum with theirs.

Carl released his hold on me and swatted my ass playfully. "Damn. That is so much better than pussy! Much tighter and you really know how to milk a man's cock, let me tell you that," Carl purred. I was pretty sure those words were intended for Jayden who still sat on the sofa appearing transfixed by the final moments of the football game playing out on the television screen.

I slipped away and headed down the hall to the bathroom for a quick shower. Jamie had hung fresh towels on shower curtain rod, and when I emerged from the bathroom my sweat shirt and sweat pants were lying outside of the bathroom door. I pulled them on and returned to the living room where the others had dressed and were now lounging around, drinking beer, and watching the final moments of the lopsided game ending on the television.

As soon as the game ended, Jayden jumped to his feet and announced he had to leave for home. He thanked Carl for inviting him and Jamie for hosting. He nodded in the direction of Brad and me when he said, "Catch you guys later," and then he bolted for the door.

"I think we scared him," I said when I was sure he was out of hearing.

"I doubt that," Carl laughed, "I wonder if he will make it all the way home before he starts jerking off or if he will pull off the road and finish the job there."

"No need to take that load home," Jamie added with a smirk.

Brad joined their laughter, then turned to me and explained, "Jayden's wife won't have anything to do with him when she is pregnant. Apparently, the first time she got pregnant she miscarried the morning after they had done the wild thing, and now she is convinced that any sexual contact will be harmful to the unborn baby."

"So that means Jayden has been sitting on the sidelines for nearly seven months now. I'm surprised his hand isn't calloused or his balls haven't literally exploded by now," Carl added.

"You don't think he will run his mouth at school, do you?" I asked, imagining what that would do to the job security of all of us.

"No," Carl assured, "Don't worry about that. Jayden is not going to say a word, and he will be back next week. "

"He kept trying not to watch what was going on, but I caught him staring at us several times when we were all around the ottoman," Jamie said with a grin. "I'd say his appetite has been whetted."

The conversation drifted to other topics and eventually Brad and I took our leave and headed home. Brad took my hand as we were leaving, and I noticed Carl raise his eyebrows in response.

"Enjoy yourself?" Brad asked once we were alone in his car and leaving the subdivision.

"Yeah, did you?"

"It was cool. But I would have preferred to come inside of you," he grinned.

"Well, I think that can be arranged when we get home," I told him. And it was.

CHAPTER FIFTEEN

The school was an absolute madhouse during the week before the playoff games began. Every club was encouraged to create a banner to support the team, and a pep rally was held on Friday to bolster the team's confidence and, let's face it, increase ticket sales for the game. My association with football coaches had revealed the reason football was considered a holy cow in most high schools: it was a cash cow. A successful season could bring in over a million dollars in revenue for the school.

Carl had already announced that a party would be held on Sunday at Jamie's place regardless of the outcome of the game. If they won, it would be a celebration of their victory. If the team lost, it would be a celebration of a successful season. Carl had not invited me to his office for his "hump day" suck and fuck sessions for weeks now, and Brad was reporting that Carl's wife was making sure his needs were met Monday through Thursday nights. I did not ask how he had gained this insight. I was pretty sure I did not want to know.

Friday night found me sitting on a cold bleacher rooting for the team along with what felt like half of the county. Everyone who had ever played football for the school seemed to be in attendance; many of them stuffed into their old varsity jackets which were now about twenty sizes too small for them to button. I knew Brad would not expect me to comment on the game, so I used the time to people watch. Both fathers and mothers played the role of sideline coach, screaming encouragement to their son and yelling advice to the coaches when they were not yelling derogatory remarks at the opposing team. We could definitely kiss any kind of sportsmanship accommodation goodbye after this game. The fathers were bad, but the mothers were worse. I now understood why some of the players behaved the way they did in the halls and classrooms.

To put it bluntly, we were outmatched as I suspect Carl had anticipated, and we got our butts kicked all over the field. Instead of winning, the goal eventually became keeping the final score from looking like a basketball routing. When the clock ran out, there was no joy in Mudville.

Back home, I waited for Brad to show up. I knew it would be late because after a loss like this one the coaches would hold the players and talk it out until they felt the players' emotions were under control. When the door opened and Brad walked in, I handed him a cold beer and Boozer pounced on his leg demanding immediate attention.

"Well, today was a double whammy," Brad sighed as he sank onto the sofa.

"How so?"

"My roommate got the job; he'll be moving over Christmas," Brad explained between swigs of beer. "Which means I either have to fork over double the rent in order to keep my apartment, or find a new roommate or a new apartment."

"Is the rent that high?"

"It is when you are paying off as many student loans as I still have going. My parents contributed nothing toward the cost of college. They really couldn't, but they also didn't want to," Brad said, looking at the floor, not at me. I knew this was a sensitive subject. He had rarely even mentioned his parents to me before tonight. I had not even been sure they were still alive. I decided it was best not to probe; if he wanted to continue, he would.

"I worked multiple jobs every summer and at least two part time jobs during the school year to keep from borrowing any more than I had to, but the loans were still huge. When I got out and got this job, I set up my payback schedule with the idea of paying them off as fast as possible, so what I pay each month is more than the minimum, but it will shave years off the total. I wasn't thinking about living by myself and having to deal with all of the expenses alone. Then I spent a huge amount of my savings on the wedding preparations. Well, let's just say that is money I will never see again. So now I just need to deal with it, you know. I mean, it will work out okay; I just didn't really need to have the extra stress thrown on me today."

"Move forward a bit," I directed, and he slid out onto the edge of the sofa. I maneuvered so I could get behind him and straddle his back. He leaned forward and I started to gently massage his shoulders and work my way up and down his spine, mixing up the three or four massage movements I knew.

"That feels so good," he sighed, "but hold up." He rose from the sofa and headed toward the stairs. "Don't move," he said, "I'll be right back." Boozer traipsed up the stairs after him, and a few minutes later I heard Brad's footsteps echoed by Boozer's toenails returning down the stairs. Brad was shirtless and held the bottle of massage oil in his hand. He handed the bottle to me, then he returned to his position between my legs. "You may continue," he purred. I poured some oil on his back and began again, gently kneading his neck and shoulders which were tight with stress. Rubbing my thumbs in a circular motion I trailed down each side of his spine to stimulate blood flow to the tissues beneath his skin.

"Somebody passed advanced anatomy," Brad observed when I

started stroking his back, following the line of each muscle group.

"Yup. I had visions of being a doctor before I settled for being a teacher."

"I wouldn't call that 'settling.' What you do impacts a lot of kids' lives," Brad said, turning to look over his shoulder at me.

"I know."

"Will you go with me to look at apartments?" Brad asked.

"Sure. But right now I think the best move would be for both of us to get to bed."

Reluctantly Brad rose from the sofa and took Boozer to the back door for a final chance to water the backyard. I began the process of turning off lights and locking doors. Finally we were both up the stairs and in bed. Brad lay on his side with Boozer snuggled up next to his stomach. I nestled in behind Brad and wrapped my arm over his ribcage. He grasped my hand and pulled it up closer to his heart, and that was the last thing I remember before we both drifted into sleep.

When I awoke the next morning, it was nearly noon. Brad was already downstairs with the Saturday paper spread across the kitchen table. The sports section was lying face down on the table in the discard pile—I figured the cover story was about our disappointing loss in the regional game. Normally, Brad would be at school for practice and a review of the previous night's game, but since the season was now officially over, there was no need for such a meeting. Monday's regularly scheduled practice would suffice for turning in uniforms and gear.

Brad barely looked up when I entered the room, but his voice greeted me as I scoured the refrigerator for ideas for brunch. "Good afternoon, sleepy head," he joked as he flipped another page in the paper. "Just grab a yogurt or something light because I am taking you out to eat as soon as we both shower and get dressed."

"What's the special occasion?" I asked while pouring a glass of orange juice.

"Apartment shopping! I have already called four people about listings in this morning's paper. I have appointments to look at three of them this afternoon."

An hour later we were seated at a booth in a local dive renowned for its breakfast buffet. On the weekends, it became a brunch buffet, and Brad and I barely arrived in time to scoop food onto our plates before the wait staff started to transform it into their dinner buffet line. We both consumed far too many calories and would spend hours at the gym sometime next week trying to atone for this sin, but every bite of scrambled eggs with cheddar cheese, homemade biscuits doused in honey and real butter, bacon, and fried potatoes with onions was worth the penance we would have to pay.

The first apartment was not in a bad neighborhood; it was in a neighborhood that would have to undergo a tremendous amount of reformation to come up to the level of "bad." There appeared to be an equal ratio of pit bulls to humans, and I suspected we could purchase just about anything on the stoop of the apartment house where we were being shown a "garden" apartment. The landlord led us down the hallway and then up a back staircase to a door that looked like a good push could suffice instead of a key. Inside, there were literally holes punched through the plasterboard in both the living room and the bedroom.

"Of course, those will be patched before you take possession," the landlord assured us.

Most of the kitchen cabinets were missing either door handles or doors, and the refrigerator was a burnt gold number straight from the 1970's when I figured this building had been erected. No mention was made by the landlord of replacing the cabinet doors and hardware or of upgrading the appliances. There was no light bulb in the miniscule bathroom, and I suspected I knew why. The accumulated mildew and rust would be a surprise for whoever signed the contract and took possession of the key to this lovely place. This was not actually a garden apartment since it had a separate bedroom, but I did not point out that inconsistency to the owner. I figured he thought the amount of dirt ground into the wall to wall shag carpet qualified it as a garden of some sort. The red bulb in the bedroom ceiling gave me a pretty good idea about the last vegetation grown here.

The second apartment was in a much better neighborhood. It was actually a basement apartment in a private residence. The elderly lady who lived there with her bedridden husband met us on the front porch of the home and then escorted us around the house and down a sloping walkway consisting of flagstones to the back door of the walk-out basement. We stepped inside to find a huge "L" shaped open space. The kitchen area was defined by a countertop bar with stools that served as both preparation area and eating space. A twelve foot square rug implied a living room area complete with a cable television connection on one wall. The foot of the "L" was recessed from view when one first entered the door to the apartment, and I assumed that was to be the bedroom area since the bathroom door opened off of one side. The bathroom, indeed the entire space, was spotless and all of the appliances were practically brand new. The couple had remodeled the house to create the apartment when their granddaughter had chosen to attend the local college and wanted to live off of campus. She had graduated last spring, the lady explained, and had recently gotten a job offer and moved to another city. That was why the apartment was now available.

Back in the car, Brad and I discussed the apartment. We both agreed the space was great, but there were drawbacks. How receptive would an elderly couple be of a gay boarder in their basement? Brad did not plan on organizing gay pride marches in the basement, but he also did not want to hide his sexual preference from people any longer. The lady had hinted, more than once, that it would be nice to have a nice, strong man around the house should she need help with anything. Brad was afraid that living in this situation would be too much like living with his parents—hiding his sexuality and being at their beck and call every time they needed something fixed or moved.

The third apartment was located overtop of a storefront on Main Street. The bottom floor was occupied by a very successful Chinese restaurant. "Take-out will be a cinch," I had observed when we pulled up to the curb in front of the building. A beautifully restored solid wood door to the right of the restaurant's windows led to the second and third floor apartments. The jovial woman who met us on the sidewalk in front of the building explained that she and her husband had purchased the building a decade earlier when the building was in disrepair and the price of real estate on Main Street was at an all time low due to both merchants and shoppers flocking to the mall. They had restored all of the apartments on the second floor and were slowly working on the units on the third floor "as time and money become available."

The door to the apartment opened into the kitchen which featured new appliances and beautiful solid wood cabinetry. The living area was about twice the size of the kitchen; still, there would not be room for a sofa and a love seat both—not if one wanted to walk between them. French doors off one side of the living room revealed a bedroom large enough for a twin bed and a dresser or a full size bed and no dresser. The space was small. The rent was not. Still, the owner seemed very anxious for Brad to rent the place. He had every quality she was looking for: he was young, attractive, and he had a guaranteed source of income.

Back in the car, Brad sighed, "Strike three."

"Cheer up! There are other options," I said as I gave his thigh a squeeze.

"Yeah," he moaned, "I can always post an ad for a roommate. Let's see, how should I word that? Wanted: reliable roommate to share a two bedroom apartment in a good neighborhood. Split rent and all utilities. Lots of closet space because I just came out of one."

I laughed. "I don't think you have to go that far just yet. After all, you have until the end of December to find something."

"Maybe I'll just suck it up and pay the full rent until my contract runs out in July. I'm going to lose my security deposit if I leave earlier than that. It'll be tight, but I can manage it."

"Dinner is on me tonight," I announced as I swung into the grocery store parking lot.

"Literally or figuratively?" Brad quipped.

"Figuratively."

"Damn," he grinned, "I was hoping we were stopping for a can of whipped cream."

An hour later we stood at my kitchen counter constructing taco salads and popping the tops off of Coronas. Dinner was served in the living room in front of the television while emergency room doctors performed all manner of operations on needy and often vituperative patients. Later, I slipped upstairs to begin my cleansing ritual in preparation for the next day. Brad remained on the sofa cuddling with Boozer.

A little before midnight, we called it a night and slid under the covers of the king-sized bed, snuggling together near its center. Brad fell asleep long before I did. My mind was racing, weighing the pros and cons of the notion that had started forming in my mind the moment Brad first told me his roommate might be getting a promotion and leaving town. In the years since my partner had died, I had come to value my privacy, my personal space and independence. I had also come to value Brad. Our relationship had developed much faster and much stronger than I had ever imagined possible, and a part of me still kept waiting for the other shoe to drop, but no negative side was I finding to this arrangement. Brad spent more time in my house than he did in his apartment, yet I never felt encroached upon; in fact, when he was not there, I found myself longing for him. By the time I finally fell asleep I had reached a decision; I fell asleep confident that it was the right decision for both of us.

CHAPTER SIXTEEN

Carl was right. Jayden was back. When Brad and I walked through the front door of Jamie's townhouse, Jayden met us bearing two cold beers. "Here's to a hell of a season," he laughed, "Thank God it's over!" Jayden plopped down on the sofa and motioned for Brad and I to join him. Carl was sprawled out on the other end, and Jamie was still puttering around in the kitchen. The TV was tuned to some sports channel, but the volume was down so low that it was practically inaudible. It didn't take long for me to realize Jayden was working on his third or fourth beer and was feeling no pain. I had never seen him this high spirited nor this talkative.

"Don't get me wrong," Jayden explained, "I loved every minute of it, but it will be nice to have a life in the evenings instead of going home dead tired and still having to pull hours correcting papers before bed."

Jayden turned toward me. "You know what I mean, don't ya?" he asked, slapping his hand down on my leg, "After all, you teach English."

I nodded my agreement. We were only in the first semester, and already I was sick of grading essays practically every night. The conversation drifted to other subjects, but Jayden's hand remained planted on my leg. I glanced at Brad, but he quickly averted his gaze and bit the side of his hand to avoid laughing out loud at the situation. Looking up, I noticed Carl had a shit-eating grin plastered on his face as he pretended to be mesmerized by the almost silent television coverage of some golf tournament.

"Come get it while it's hot!" Jamie yelled from the kitchen, and Carl nearly vaulted off the end of the sofa and beat a pathway to the kitchen. Brad followed, and it was only when I rose from the sofa that Jayden let his hand fall from my inner thigh.

A steaming tray of hot Buffalo wings sat on the counter beside bowls of potato salad, potato chips, pretzels, and coleslaw. A crock pot held pulled pork barbeque and a loaf of Hawaiian sweet bread had been carved into a bowl and filled with spinach dip.

We each loaded our plates and headed back into the living room. Carl and Jamie had already claimed the shorter end of the sectional sofa, so Brad, Jayden, and I once again took the longer side. Since the conversation at these parties always centered around sports and I knew absolutely nothing about the subject, I spent a lot of time trying to look interested without contributing much to the conversation. By the time the football game began, plates had been cleared and deposited in the kitchen, and fresh beers had been pulled from the fridge.

Jayden's leg was plastered against mine, and the warmth from the contact was making me extremely horny. I had wondered for years what this man looked like sans clothing, and I was hoping that tonight might be a fantasy come true. Jayden seemed very friendly, and drunk, and I figured the alcohol consumption was his way of getting past the inhibitions that had kept him plastered to the sofa last week while everyone else stripped naked and proceeded to get off.

When halftime came, everyone headed to the kitchen for refills, and I noticed Jayden got quiet and seemed nervous. Third quarter was generally when the sex started unless the game was close and everyone really wanted to watch the action. I suspected Carl, who orchestrated every move, intentionally chose games that he knew were going to be one-sided so that there would be no need to watch breathlessly. At halftime, the score for this game was already very lopsided and even the announcers were using the term "blowout" during their analysis.

About ten minutes into the second half, Carl stuck his hand under the elastic band of his pants and began stroking his cock. Brad and Jamie followed his lead, and finally even Jayden's right hand had slipped into his sweats and was busy.

Carl stood and toed off his shoes. He shucked his sweatpants to the floor and stepped out of them. Facing the TV, he continued stroking his now turgid cock with slow leisurely strokes. Brad stood and began pulling off his shirt and sweats. Jamie shed his shirt, then stood to remove his shorts. I joined the action, standing and slowly taking off my shirt and then my sweatpants and shoes. Jayden pulled off his shoes, but remained on the sofa, stroking his cock inside of his sweatpants.

I moved in front of Carl and dropped to my knees; I took his cock in my hand and began slowly stroking it. I flicked my tongue over the piss slit, then engulfed the head in my mouth and swirled my tongue around it before slowly moving down his shaft until my face nuzzled his pubic hair and his cock entered my throat. I kneaded his cock with my tongue before sliding back to the head. Carl moaned and I began rapidly sucking his cock, the thick shaft gliding in and out of my throat as I grasped his ass cheeks in my hands and slowly squeezed them, feeling his muscles tense beneath my touch. Carl's moans grew louder until he lightly pushed against my forehead with his palm. I let his cock slip from my mouth and stood.

The ottoman was in place and covered with a sheet. I felt a hand on my ass and turned to find Brad standing behind me, the bottle of lube open in his right hand, his left hand easing between my ass cheeks to lube my hole. I pushed my ass back and he slipped his hand down my crack and inserted a finger into my tight hole. He worked it slightly, then inserted a second finger and began finger fucking me. I bent over to give him greater access. To my surprise, he knelt behind me, spread my cheeks with his hands, and planted his mouth over my hole. His tongue darted into my hole and a moan escaped my lips. Jamie stepped in front of me and offered his cock. I could not grab it with my hands as I was using them on my knees for balance, but he held his cock steady and I slid the large shaft down my throat and began sucking him in rhythm to Brad's fingers fucking my ass.

"Damn, that's hot," I heard Jayden say. I could not see him, so he had to be behind me somewhere.

"Is he ready?" Carl asked, and Brad came up for air and apparently indicated in the affirmative because Jamie pushed my face off of his cock and motioned to the ottoman. I turned around and sat on the ottoman and leaned backward. Jamie grabbed my right ankle and Brad took my left ankle. They raised my legs into the air toward my chest and held them while Carl stepped into place. Carl grabbed my hips and pulled me slightly toward him before placing the tip of his cock against my hole and pushing it in to the hilt in one slick motion. He ground his groin against my ass to gain maximum penetration and then slowly pulled back to the point where only the head of his cock remained inside of me.

"Today," he proclaimed, grinning, "We celebrate the end of a great season, and the beginning of a newfound brotherhood. Let the rites of initiation begin." And with his final word, he began to plow my ass hard and fast, his balls slapping against my ass with each deep stroke. He was wasting no time and making no effort to prolong his climax. His head was thrown back and his eyes closed as he pounded deeper and faster on each thrust. Finally, he buried his cock deep within my ass and he omitted a sound that seemed like a cross between a yell and a moan. I began milking his cock with my ass muscles, draining every drop of cum from his rigid cock. He gasped and his body shook as he gripped my hips harder and pushed even further into my hole. I could tell a second load of cum had just erupted from his cock, and then his shoulders rolled forward and he went limp from head to toe. He slowly withdrew his spent cock from my ass, instructing Jamie and Brad to pull my legs higher so as not to allow his spunk to seep from my dripping hole. Carl moved beside of Brad and took hold of my ankle.

"He's your lover. You should be next," he instructed.

Brad moved into position between my splayed legs and leaned over to plant a hot, tongue-filled kiss on my lips. Straightening, he positioned his cock against my hole and asked, "You ready?"

"Hell yes," I whispered hoarsely, "Fuck me deep and hard."

Brad slammed his cock forward, impaling me on his shaft. I gasped in surprise, but urged him on. He quickly established a rhythm equal to Carl and the sound of his nads slapping my ass on every down stroke echoed in the room. I realized someone had muted the TV.

"Let me hear how much you want him," Carl urged.

"Fuck me, Brad; fuck me hard," I moaned. Brad pounded harder, his cock a piston moving fluidly in and out of my slippery hole. "That feels so damned good," I yelled, "give it to me. Fill me with your seed. Breed this ass!"

Brad's face contorted and he wrapped his arms around my knees and pumped as hard and fast as he could, his strokes shorter now, his breath coming in gasps. Finally he let forth an inarticulate sound of release and slammed his cock deep within me. His body trembled as I milked his throbbing cock of its load. I was careful though not to bring him off a second time. I was being selfish—I wanted that second load at home tonight just before falling to sleep in his protective embrace.

Again Carl and Jamie pulled my legs upward as Brad's cock slid free. Bra d took Jamie's place and Jamie hesitantly stepped between my legs.

"Give it to me," I commanded, making direct eye contact with him. "Ride this ass and blast that load inside me."

Jamie edged forward until his cock was against my hole.

"Do it!" I demanded.

He closed his eyes and slammed his cock deep inside of me. He gasped as his groin ground against my ass, then he began fucking me in deep furious strides. He grabbed my knees and pummeled my ass like it was an enemy he was trying to overcome. His eyes stayed tightly closed and perspiration beaded on his forehead as he pounded harder and harder into my hole. Finally, he threw his head back and yelled, "OHHHHHH FUCCCCCCCCK!!" as wave after wave of cum flooded my ass. Each time I tightened my ass muscles around his cock, a fresh burst of cum erupted from his dick and his body convulsed as he gasped. Releasing his hold on my knees, he stepped back as Brad and Carl pulled my legs upwards again to retain the loads that had been deposited inside of me.

I had forgotten about Jayden. He had not been in my sightline and had not spoken since Brad had been rimming my ass at the beginning of this initiation rite. So I was a bit surprised when he appeared between my legs, his caramel skin gleaming under a sheen of perspiration, his pectorals hard and round above a solid abdomen. Soft tightly curled hair sprinkled across his chest thickened over his breastbone and formed a dark trail that led down to a dense nap at his groin. He was holding his cock in his left hand, and I am sure my eyes widened at the sight of it. Jayden's cock was rock hard and huge. Thicker than the beer cans we had been holding earlier and bullet shaped, it reminded me of an artillery shell. Not only did the man have girth, he had length—about nine or ten inches. I was suddenly damned glad the other men had loosened me up to take this monster cock.

"And now for the new initiate," Carl grinned, "Are you sure you are up for this? This ass is a man-eater. It's not for the faint of heart."

"Neither is this dick," Jayden intoned, locking eyes with me. "Are you sure you can handle this?"

"Bring it on!" I commanded.

Jayden inched forward until the head of his cock pushed against my hole. Unlike the others, who had entered fast and deep, Jayden pushed steadily and slowly buried his huge cock inside of my hungry ass.

"You good?" he asked once he was firmly embedded within me. Brad and Carl had relaxed their grip on my ankles, giving me a bit more control over my own response. I humped my ass up against his cock, driving him further inside of me, grinding my ass against his thick bush.

"All right then," he grinned, and began to slowly slide his cock back and forth within me. Each stroke was longer than the one before it until he was pulling back to the tip of his cock and then thrusting full force deep into my ass.

"Give me his legs," he growled, and Carl and Brad relinquished them at once, stepping back to watch as Jayden took full control of my body. Pulling my legs up against his torso, so that my feet were on either side of his head, he grabbed me around the thighs and began to pump his cock into me in increasingly rapid strokes. The rate of his pounding increased until his face began to contort and his breathing became rapid and audible. I began squeezing his cock with my ass muscles every time he started to withdraw, and the effect was immediate. "Holy shit!" he exclaimed, as he slammed deeper into me, his big nuts slapping loudly against my ass. "You're gonna make me cum!"

"Fuck me, stud!" I stage whispered, "Give me all of that big cock! Make that ass serve you! Breed me, baby, breed me. Plant that hot load deep inside of me. You know you want to mix your load with

Carl's cum, and Jamie's cum, and Brad's cum. Can't you feel their semen coating your big cock and making it all slippery as you pound this ass? Breed me, stud! Breed me now!" And with that I clinched my ass tightly around his pole as he thrust it deep inside of me. He pushed hard against me as his load erupted from his monster cock and creamed my insides. I milked his big cock as well as I could with my ass muscles until I was sure I had every drop of his load and I could feel his cock soften inside of me.

Jamie and Brad grabbed my legs and pulled them up near my head as Jayden withdrew his cock from my ass. Carl stepped behind me. He slipped his right index finger deep inside of my dripping hole and withdrew it. It glistened with the comingled cum of the four men who had just fucked me. Carl held his finger up and looked at it before moving it to his lips and sucking off the glistening fluid. Moving to my side, he relieved Jamie of duty by taking my ankle from him. Jamie moved between my legs and inserted his finger, withdrew it, and licked it clean. Carl signaled to Jayden, who was still breathing heavy. Jayden likewise inserted a finger and withdrew it gleaming with seminal fluid. He sucked the substance off of his finger and then smacked his lips in appreciation. Jamie took my ankle from Brad, and Brad moved between my legs. He looked me in the eye and then grinned before he dropped to his knees and buried his face in my ass. He lapped at my quivering hole and darted his tongue in and out as I tried to clinch my ass and hold his tongue inside of me. Finally, he withdrew and stood, his lips and chin glistening. Carl and Jamie lowered my legs to the floor, but Brad remained between my legs, and when I started to push myself up, he placed a hand in the center of my chest to stop me.

"We're not done, men." He said. "Not everyone has dropped a load."

Brad knelt between my legs and took my cock in his hand, It was rigid and he slid his hand to the base and then began lapping, licking, and sucking on the mushroom head. With his free hand he reached up and began gently to play with my nipple. Jayden moved in close beside of me and began to roll my other nipple between his fingertips, mimicking Brad's movements.

"Suck it," Brad instructed. "It's just like a woman's tit—just flat chested."

Jayden lowered his lips to my nipple and began to gently suck it and lap it with his tongue. I squirmed in pleasure as one hunky man sucked my cock and another one sucked my nipple. Brad hoisted my legs up over his shoulders and focused on the blow job he was giving my cock. Carl knelt beside of me and pushed Brad's hand off of my other nipple. He bent down and began sucking it and flicking his tongue across the top. This was getting to be more stimulation than I could take. My hips were bucking up, face fucking Brad as he sucked my cock. My torso twisted and I gasped and moaned from the sensation of having both nipples sucked by two handsome men about whom I had fantasized for years. Jamie dropped on to his knees beside of Brad and snaked a hand under my butt and began to finger fuck my ass, rubbing on my prostate. That was the last straw.

"I'm. . .going . . .to . . .cum!" I gasped.

Brad released my cock and tilted it toward my chest just as the huge globules of cum spurted out and landed on my abdomen and chest. At least one spray caught Carl on the side of his face. He wiped it off with his finger, then licked the sticky substance from his finger. Jayden dipped his face toward my abdomen and licked a stream of cum from my ribcage. Carl stood to give Jamie room as Jamie scooted around to my side and licked a glob of cum from my stomach.

"The rest is mine, fellas," Brad purred as he leaned over me and with long laps of his tongue cleaned my chest and abs of the load I had just blown.

"Well, I can honestly say I've never done that before," Carl shrugged with a sly grin.

"Me either," Jamie admitted. "Always wondered what cum would taste like, but never had the guts to taste my own much less someone else's."

"I sure as hell hope I don't regret this tomorrow," Jayden said as he searched the pile of discarded clothes, "when I am sober."

"Thank you, gentlemen," I said as Brad helped me to my feet. "Time to clean up," I announced as I headed toward the hallway. Brad followed me down the hallway to the bathroom and stepped inside the tub with me. While we lathered each other with soap in the shower, the other three men were using the sink to wash themselves and towel dry before traipsing back to the living room to get dressed.

By the time Brad and I joined them, Jamie was fully dressed and in the kitchen retrieving a beer. Carl and Jayden were searching through the remaining clothing looking for Jayden's underwear. Jayden explained what they were doing and then added with a shy smile, "It is absolutely imperative that I return home in my own damned underwear or you won't have to worry about this happening again because she will fucking kill me."

Eventually Jayden's boxers were found and he dressed and left. Jamie was puttering around in the kitchen putting food away, leaving Carl, Brad and I in the living room. Carl was sprawled on the end of the sofa, one leg draped over the arm and the other on the floor. Brad was standing idly watching the post-game discussion by the sportscasters on TV while I finished lacing up my shoes.

Brad turned to Carl and said, "So now you know."

Carl smiled slightly and responded, "I've known for a while now, stud. The two of you are hot together." He paused, then added, "Don't fuck it up, or I just might divorce the bitch I am married to and move in with him myself."

"You know you love pussy," Brad countered with a grin.

"Yeah, but now I love man pussy too," Carl said with a wide smile. "When do I get to test yours?"

"Everything in due time," Brad purred. "You'll have to get permission from my man before you can tap this ass."

"Whoa! I guess we know who wears the pants in this relationship!" Carl said laughing.

"Yeah," Brad responded slyly, "We both do."

CHAPTER SEVENTEEN

When we returned to my townhouse that night, Brad immediately collapsed on the sofa with the remote control. Boozer joined him. I went into the kitchen and popped a frozen lasagna into the oven for dinner, and then I returned to the living room and sat cross-legged in the brown chair.

"We need to talk," I said when a commercial filled the TV screen.

"Oh shit," Brad groaned. He pushed the mute button on the remote control and sat up. His posture screamed insecurity—legs crossed at the ankles, arms folded across his chest, head bowed, staring into his lap. Boozer sensed the change in mood and crawled into Brad's lap to divert his attention from whatever might be making him sad.

"Don't get uptight. It's nothing bad."

"It's just that is how I broke the news to my fiancée."

I laughed and he looked at me like I was the most insensitive fool on earth.

"Are you gonna break up with me?" he asked, his voice choking back emotion.

"Hell no!" I exclaimed. "I'm asking you to move in with me."

It took a moment for my words to register with him. Then he stared at me for at least a minute before he said anything at all.

"Are you serious?"

"Totally," I confirmed.

"You mean, like pack all of my shit and move it over here?" He stood up and walked to the chair. "You mean, no more hunting for an apartment?" He knelt in front of me. "You mean, living together as a couple, and holding hands in public, and taking one car to work every day, and going to movies together, and kissing in the mall if we feel like it, and making vacation plans together?"

I nodded my head.

"Are you sure you are ready for that?" he asked.

"No. But I am willing to try. We will never know how it feels to be a real couple until we start acting like one. No hiding, no holding back, no playing it safe. I've spent too many years avoiding feeling anything. I want to take the risk of getting hurt if it means I also have a chance at spending every day of the rest of my life wrapped in your arms." I cupped his face in my hands. "Are you ready for that?"

"I don't know. But I sure as hell want to try." His face lit up in a smile. He perched on the wide arm of the chair and closed in for a kiss. It would have been very romantic if Boozer had not started howling at the top of his lungs and then tried hurling himself at the chair in an attempt to come between us.

"Relax dude," Brad comforted the dog as he stroked his long ears, "I'm in love with you both."

The next hour or so was spent working out logistics. Brad's roommate was leaving in December. We would begin moving Brad's stuff a little at a time over the next week or so. Most of the furniture in Brad's apartment belonged to the roommate, so there was not much to move beyond personal items. Brad's bed could be stored in the guest room as could his dresser and a chair he had bought when he first moved out on his own. The rest had come from the Salvation Army thrift store and could return there.

By the time the oven dinged announcing that dinner was ready, we had a plan. Monday we would start driving to school together. If people asked, we would answer them honestly, but we would not make any kind of announcement regarding Brad's sexual preference nor our relationship. Those who needed to know would figure it out; the rest did not need to know.

That night we retired to bed a lot earlier than usual. It had been an exciting and fun day, but it had also been emotionally and physically exhausting. Clinging to each other in the middle of our king sized bed with Boozer draped across Brad's legs pouting because we would not let him sleep between us, we kissed and cuddled until sleep began to overtake us.

"I love you," I whispered, surprised at how easily the words slid off my tongue. It had been more than a decade since I had used those words with anyone other than Boozer. I wasn't even sure Brad was still awake to hear them. His eyes were closed and his breathing was deep but steady. I stroked his soft curly hair back from where it had fallen into his face and traced the outline of his jaw with one finger tip. His eyes fluttered open.

"I love you too," he whispered back. His eyes closed and within moments he was sound asleep.

I lay there for several minutes staring at this beautiful man who wanted to share his life with me, and I knew that the road ahead of us would not be easy, but then when is it ever easy to build a relationship and maintain it? I snuggled closer to Brad and entangled my fingers in his hair. Tomorrow we would wake up in each other's arms. Tomorrow we would drive to school together and enter the building through the same door. Tomorrow would be the start of a brand new adventure. And for the first time in a long time, I could not wait for tomorrow to arrive.

ABOUT THE AUTHOR

Chris Sherman was born and raised in the northern end of the Shenandoah Valley in Virginia, where he continues to make his home. He is the author of MAKING THE SALE and THE HEAD COACH'S PLAYBOOK, both gay erotic romances. He is eagerly anticipating the day when he can call writing his "real" job.

www.ingramcontent.com/pod-product-compliance
Lightning Source LLC
Chambersburg PA
CBHW051519170626
46811CB00002B/904
9780615851099